ATHA BAS CA

Harry Kleinhuis

Red Deer Press

Published in Canada by Red Deer Press, 195 Allstate Parkway, Markham, ON L3R 4T8

Published in the United States by Red Deer Press, 311 Washington Street, Brighton, MA 02135

Red Deer Press acknowledges with thanks the Canada Council for the Arts and the Ontario Arts Council for their support of our publishing program. We acknowledge the financial support of the Government of Canada through the Canada Book Fund (CBF) for our publishing activities.

Edited for the Press by Peter Carver
Text and cover design by Tanya Montini
Proudly printed in Canada by Houghton Boston

Library and Archives Canada Cataloguing in Publication
Title: Athabasca / Harry Kleinhuis.
Names: Kleinhuis, Harry, 1943- author.
Identifiers: Canadiana 2020036197X | ISBN 9780889956346 (softcover)
Classification: LCC PS8621.L45 A84 2021 | DDC jC813/.6—dc23

Publisher Cataloging-in-Publication Data (U.S.)
Names: Kleinhuis, Harry, 1943-, author.
Title: Athabasca / Harry Kleinhuis.
Description: Markham, Ontario : Red Deer Press, 2021.| Summary: "Jack is 14 going on 15. He lives with his family on the Athabasca River. It's the late 1930s, and the river is still wild and untamed. Jack, as a teenager, is in conflict with his parents and decides to take out on his own by canoeing down the river. Trouble is, on the first day, he breaks his arm, and has to stay stranded, alone, unable to go further. His father follows and finds him and somehow father and son begin to communicate in ways they never have. All of this is played out against the backdrop of a powerful river where nature is dominant and where a family manages their lives alone in the bush, with little or no reference to the world beyond." -- Provided by publisher.
Identifiers: ISBN 978-0-88995-634-6 (paperback)
Subjects: LCSH Teenagers – Family relationships—Juvenile fiction. | Athabasca River (Alta.) – Juvenile fiction. | BISAC: YOUNG ADULT FICTION / Family / Parents.
Classification: LCC PZ7.K645Ath |DDC [F] – dc23

www.reddeerpress.com

To all those who sit by a campfire at night
to talk and sort things out.
Preferably beside a big adventurous river
that is taking them to somewhere.

PART 1

1

Jack sat up on the high bluffs above the river and watched the dark patches of ice float by. It was late spring. He knew it was almost time. Time for a lot of things. Time for the river to settle down after the run-off. Time for his dad to link up with Mr. Harley a little farther upstream, for their run up to the trading post in Hinton. Time for him to wait a few more days after that, and then head out as well. But only he knew anything about that.

From this spot above the river—his lookout, as he called it— Jack had watched the big Athabasca River for seven years, and in all seasons. On good summer days, in the sunshine, when the wind blew from the southwest, he'd watched the bald eagles rise up and circle and soar, looking for their target, their opportunity, and their time to thunder down out of the skies on some unsuspecting prey below. That was how they lived. And survived.

For seven years Jack had watched and learned. He'd waited, soared, hovered, and sensed the air and the currents that wove their way through his life. He was waiting for his own day to do what he knew he had to do.

Seven years had been a long time for Jack. But not for the big Athabasca River in its long and twisted valley.

Seven years is not a long time for the foothill regions of the Rocky Mountains.

Seven years was only a long time for Jack. A really long time. It was half his lifetime. Seven years that he remembered well. Seven years of growing up into this time, when he knew he was ready.

Jack looked up into the blue darkness of the clear sky straight above him, beyond where the eagles could fly. He squeezed his eyes shut and wondered. Then he looked down to the sky's distant haziness near the horizon. He knew the eagles would soon be back, like always. But they would have no more to teach him, and he knew he would not be there to learn from them anymore.

Jack unfolded his teenage legs, and rose to leave the peace and sanctuary of his own secret lookout above the Athabasca, and the whispering of its currents, and the now infrequent grinding of some of the ice that still floated by from somewhere. The ice and the river still cooled the occasional rush of wind that swept up to Jack's bluffs and into the poplars, spruce, and pine trees beyond.

He didn't hurry. He was reluctant to leave. And equally reluctant to go back to what he knew awaited him.

2

From his river lookout, it was almost a quarter-mile up to the little plateau where Jack's dad, Malcolm Whyte, had built the log house for his family seven years before. It wasn't pretty. But Jack knew his dad hadn't been concerned about keeping up with the neighbors, or of offending them. He'd done what he could with the spruce logs cut from the trees close at hand. It was a practical source of building material that, at the same time, allowed him to clear a larger patch of land on the plateau for his crude homestead. The clearing provided a place to grow things, and it was a way to let in some sunlight to that isolated sanctuary to which the Whytes had retreated.

The roof of that squat little house seemed to rise out of the spring green of that grassy clearing, as Jack climbed up out of the river woods. The roof was straight and square. Probably because it was made from the boards Malcolm Whyte had salvaged from the big, clumsy wooden scow that had carried them downriver from the coal mining town of Brûlé. It had carried them as far as necessary, and had then become the roof of the family's house.

Jack remembered that. He remembered that first summer, and his mom crying as they'd taken the scow apart and carried those big boards up the hill, to where his dad had already laid out the first tier of logs for their house. Jack remembered helping. He'd been big enough to drag some of the smaller boards. He remembered the slivers. He remembered himself crying, too, and sweating, and swatting at mosquitoes, and dropping those boards when too many of those damn mosquitoes bit all at once.

Jack had wondered in that first summer why his mom had only cried at the bottom of the hill, down by the river. He'd thought it was the heavy work and the mosquitoes. But, over the years, he realized it was because of the scow itself. It had brought them to this place, but it would never carry them out. Not back up the river and through its currents to where they had come from. Not them as a family.

When you're not quite eight, you don't think about those things. You haven't seen enough of life to know how it all fits together. You don't remember the beginning, and you can't imagine the end. You only see the day you're in, when you're small. And you do what you're told to do.

But this was another year. And Jack Whyte wasn't small anymore.

3

"Dad's starting to get the furs ready."

Jack was walking past the garden on his way back to the house. Cyril, his younger brother and the next oldest at thirteen, was tilling the garden with the family's only shovel.

"Yeah, I knew he would be," Jack mumbled by way of reply. "The river's almost ready, too. Not much ice still floating by."

Getting the furs ready was the signal that the busy and critical time of the year was about to start. It was the time when Malcolm Whyte linked up with Mr. Harley for the yearly trip upriver to Hinton. They went up there to sell their winter harvest of furs, and pick up whatever supplies that sale would allow. One payday and one big shopping trip for the whole year.

"He's been calling," Cyril called after Jack. "You were gone a long time."

Jack knew that last part was a warning. He acknowledged by saying, "Yeah" over his shoulder. He didn't say why he'd been gone so long. To do that would be to reveal what he'd been thinking about. But Cyril wouldn't understand such things. Not yet. However, Jack knew Cyril's day would come, too, soon enough.

Malcolm Whyte was busy with the furs out by the shed. Checking them, counting them, and sorting them by grade and variety. There were a lot of beaver this year. Winter had been good for that. But Jack knew it was the mink that usually fetched the best price.

"Where in hell have you been?" Malcolm snarled at Jack, as soon as he heard his footsteps come up behind him.

"You told me to check the river."

Jack had learned how to be surly over the last winter. He'd learned to talk back in a tone to match his dad's. Maybe it had something to do with his growing too fast, and all the other changes that went along with that. Things nobody bothered to explain, and things he'd considered too private to ask about. Things he hadn't really been able to figure out on his own, no matter how hard and how long he thought about them. He guessed that, as with so many other things, they'd fade into the background, as he continued to get older and wiser. They were the things his young eagles seemed to do in just a few months of summer.

There were a lot of other things Jack had been thinking about in the last year or so. He knew there was a big world out there. A world of which, for some reason, they were not a part. When he'd been smaller, it hadn't mattered all that much. It was all just like the stories and things he and his brother and sister were learning from their mom, in the few books from which she taught them in the evenings, and especially during the long, cold winters.

Back then, he'd been satisfied when Mom told them they were safe here; that here they were a family; here they were as rich as they wanted to be, because of the work they did, and the things they could do for themselves. In the world away from them, there was something called The Depression. Something that made people poor, and hungry, and desperate.

Those were among the things Jack Whyte thought about in a land and time—the Athabasca country of the 1930's—when children grew slowly, if they survived, and where, later on, the hardships of the seasons and other circumstances forced them to grow old all too soon.

"Clean the traps and let them dry in the sun before you oil them," Malcolm ordered Jack. Said it like Jack might not have remembered from other times.

Jack didn't answer. He just set about doing what he knew he had to do. The same job or chore as in every other spring he could remember. The traps were the family's means to an income. They needed to be in good order to do their job.

"Make sure you strip them down good," Malcolm said. "I don't want anything to leave a smell on them."

"Yeah, I know." Jack had filled the old tub with water. "I'll let them soak for a while first."

Malcolm grunted in acknowledgement. Then he added, "You can help your brother while the first lot's soaking."

Cyril and Amelia, their little sister, did most of the smiling and laughing in the Whyte family. Jack figured it was that way because they got most of the easy chores. Although he had to admit that digging the garden in the spring was not one of the easiest things to do. Especially for Cyril. He had always been skinny and pale. Even in the hot summer months.

"Why were you down at the river so long?" Cyril asked. "Were you waiting for the eagles? Or were you waiting for the rest of the ice to melt?"

"Both. And neither happened."

"Maybe Dad will let me go on the fur trip upriver someday," Cyril mused, as he tugged at a tree root that had wandered into their garden from a long way away. The shadows of the tallest trees in the area nearby didn't reach to the middle of their garden, but their roots sure did.

Jack almost laughed to watch Cyril pull on the stubborn thing, while he himself kept on working with the shovel. He knew that more roots would find their way into the garden as soon as their mom got things organized, and they spread some manure from the outhouse that got moved every year.

"Going up the Athabasca in the spring is a lot of hard work," Jack said in answer to his brother's suggestion. "Moving that heavy canoe means wading and pulling it along as much as paddling it. The top of me is usually sweating, while my legs are numb and cold from the icy water."

Cyril winced and giggled at the thought of it.

Jack noticed and snorted. "You can take my place this year if you want to. I was younger than you the first time Dad made me come along."

Actually, as he thought back to that first time, he'd been proud to have had the privilege, or responsibility. It meant doing a real man's job, even though he might not yet have been one. It also meant coming back home alone, in the smaller canoe, from the meeting place with Mr. Harley. It was like flying down the Athabasca in the currents and rapids of some of its bends and narrows. It also meant that he had learned something of the nature of the river and how it behaved, through its twists and turns, in its descent down to wherever it went.

And that may have been the beginning of his idea.

"Jack, you're going crooked! You're dreaming again!" Cyril warned him.

At the same time, there was a loud growl from the shed. "Jack! You can do this batch of traps now!"

Jack stepped out of his dreaming and gave Cyril a dirty look, as he handed back the shovel and the boots that went with the digging job. Those rubber-bottomed lace-ups were necessary when their customary bare feet couldn't handle the job. He headed back to the shed and to the growl.

"I wasn't dreaming," Jack snarled back at his little brother.

He wasn't dreaming. But neither was he ready to tell Cyril what he was thinking and planning, either. Jack knew how secrets had a way of oozing up to the surface.

One of the traps still had what was left of a mink's foot, bonded to one side of the steel trap. Jack looked at it and thought about it. He imagined one of the sleek-coated animals choosing between freedom and one of its hind feet. Maybe wrestling with the cold, unforgiving steel for much of a winter night. Jack looked for clues to how that might have unfolded. Maybe, in desperation at hearing snowshoes approaching along the trail, it had braved the pain of severing itself from the instrument that held it in its torturous grip.

Jack wondered just how much he might have to give up— how much he might lose—to gain his own freedom.

"You're dreaming!" Malcolm fired another verbal warning shot in Jack's direction.

It was only a warning this time. Maybe because Malcolm Whyte was thinking, too. His hands were beginning to shake as he pulled on the cords tightening the bales of fur.

Jack noticed but said nothing. He'd seen that sort of thing before. He'd seen it and wondered. He knew the shaking was often followed by an explosion of anger. But, more and more, he wondered if it was caused by something else. He knew his own anger had reasons behind it. Often it seemed to come from deep within.

"Do it right!" Malcolm yelled over to Jack. "Make sure there's no trace of mink blood on any of them! The smell will spook them." He said the last part more slowly, as if he'd wakened and realized where he was.

Jack didn't say anything. He'd learned not to. He'd never won an argument, because his dad had always been bigger. But not for long. He could feel it.

Jack had learned to wait. And while he waited this time, he wondered about that coming day of confrontation and, possibly, emancipation. All of which made his leaving all the more necessary. As with the Great War, Jack knew within himself that a battle right here, on the shores of the Athabasca, would certainly have losers and casualties in its outcome.

4

"Yes, I'm leaving. And you damn well better shut up about it."
Jack hissed at Cyril a few evenings later, when he told him about
his plans.

"But what will Mom and Amelia do?" Cyril whimpered.

"They'll do the same as always. And you'll be here to look
after them. You're old enough." Jack appealed to Cyril's own
sense of self-worth and skills.

Cyril was young, small, and skinny. In other circumstances,
he might have been the logical victim of any bully in a schoolyard.
But Cyril was also becoming tough and wiry.

"That's why I'm telling you this now," Jack continued. "This
way you can prepare yourself and have some answers."

"But why don't you tell them yourself? You know, when the
time comes."

Jack and his little brother were sitting up on the bluffs above
the Athabasca, at Jack's lookout. He'd invited Cyril along for this

special reason. It was an evening when there was enough of a breeze to blow the mosquitoes away. At least, most of them. The boys had been watching the river below, almost slow and quiet now, and with some gravel bars exposed.

"Because if I tell them, Mom will have arguments against it," Jack said firmly. "She'll make me feel guilty." He could think of many other reasons, but decided to keep things as simple as possible.

"But you could wait until next year. You'd be older. It would make more sense then."

"No! It has to be now!" Jack was adamant. He was starting to sound like his father. However, he did have one compelling argument. "Don't you remember Dad saying something about it being time I learned how to trap? You know, really trap?"

"Yeah. So?" Cyril looked confused. Hunting and trapping were the skills of manhood. Both he and Jack had always snared rabbits, and even set a few of the old traps in the bush up behind the house. And both of them could shoot well enough with the Cooey .22 to provide the family with meat in any season, if they had to.

"Well," Jack said, as if it was obvious, "trapping would mean going out on the trap lines with Dad, wouldn't it?"

Cyril nodded.

"And," Jack continued, "if Dad and I were both up on the trap lines for weeks at a time, what do you think might happen?"

Cyril frowned back at Jack, beginning to realize. He nodded somberly. "You and Dad argue now sometimes, don't you," he stated.

"You understand, then?" Jack asked, by way of confirmation. Neither of them had said it, but both now knew that an uncontrolled explosion of tempers would someday be inevitable. Jack wanted Cyril to know that he wanted to avoid certain disaster.

Cyril nodded again and looked down. It was the best he could do as a sign of respect for his brother's difficult decision.

"I'll tell you more before Dad and I go upstream with the furs to meet Mr. Harley," Jack said quietly. "Now let's get out of these damn flies."

5

It felt like the beginning of summer, when Malcolm checked the canoes and organized the supplies needed for the two weeks it would take for him to get the furs to Hinton, and then cruise back downstream with their household supplies for another year. He looked like he dreaded the excursion. And probably he did. Getting a good price for the furs was never a sure thing.

Jack had learned that much, too, or thought he had, as an observer and paddler on those trips for the last few years. He knew it was all or nothing. There were no options. The Depression of the thirties had whittled families and their lifestyles down to the bare and treacherous minimum. It had destroyed many in the process. If something did not succeed, there was nowhere else to turn. Like a trap, there was no escape.

Jack only helped to get his dad as far upstream as the rendezvous spot with Mr. Harley. After that, the two men helped each other when necessary. Meeting up with their neighbor, if, over such a distance, Mr. Harley could actually be called a neighbor, was a privilege for Jack. Aside from family, it was the only society he knew.

The others hovered in the background during these preparations, awaiting orders and ready to help. But not asking questions about the impossible or making suggestions. As in previous years, they knew the big canoe would return with whatever it could, and that essentials had priority. Anything beyond that would be a bonus and an unexpected surprise.

"Let's see how far we can go before we get wet," Malcolm said, with about as much optimism as he was capable of, as he ordered Jack into the bow of the big canoe, floating in the lingering mists of an early departure. They were on the inside of a long bend in the river, and could at least begin the trip upstream by paddling. The smaller canoe that Jack would need to come back from the link-up with Mr. Harley was snubbed up to the stern of the bigger canoe. There was a pole ready on top of things, for when Malcolm might need it to pole their way up some of the shallower currents that would come all too soon.

Jack knew the river well enough in the reaches up to Hinton or, at least, the place where Mr. Harley would be. He also knew that, depending on the depth of water in the changing seasons, the river's channels were not always the same. He learned by observing; he learned by working; and he learned by listening to his dad's orders about when to pull hard, when to help steer from his position in the bow, and, all too often, when to get out and pull the canoe along by wading in the always icy water.

Jack paid more attention to such river things this time. Although he'd come down solo in the little canoe from the meeting place several times, he knew that a greater adventure was going to happen. He knew that whatever he learned on this part of the river might be needed many times over, and more, on those stretches where he had never been before.

He also knew better than to ask any questions and make his dad suspicious.

He wondered what he might learn from Mr. Harley's stories at the campsite. But he didn't wonder for very long.

"Jack! Pay attention! We're going to veer across the current to the other side," Malcolm roared from the stern. "And be ready to jump out and pull the canoe when I tell you to!"

Jack felt the bow of the canoe get sucked sideways as the current caught it, and he paddled harder to keep it heading upstream. He knew what to do. He also felt stronger than he had in previous years. He was looking forward to coming back in the smaller canoe. Then, he would be boss.

6

"Mom, why don't we ever go up to Hinton and to the post?"

Amelia asked it one evening, as she helped with the cleaning up. Just blurted it out, all normal, like she was asking something as simple as when the beans might begin to sprout in the garden.

But Rose seemed to understand what Amelia was really asking. In the same way she knew those kinds of questions could only be asked when Malcolm was not close by.

"We used to live in a town," Rose said quietly.

"Brûlé," Cyril said, joining in. "We used to live in Brûlé. That's where we came from. I remember that. It was a long time ago. You were probably too small to remember."

"Broolay," Amelia said slowly, imitating her brother. Scrunching her face and trying to force out the memories.

"I don't remember much," Cyril admitted. "Just a lot of houses in rows. Real houses, with lots of windows. And a school. I remember being in Grade 1, and there were lots of books and lots of paper."

"Maybe Dad will bring us another book for our schoolwork here," Amelia said wistfully. "If there's enough money."

Cyril laughed at that. He knew what the priorities were. He also knew just how much his dad could safely handle in the big canoe.

"Jack should be home tomorrow, shouldn't he?" Amelia asked. "Tomorrow, or maybe the day after? He'll remember things about Brûlé. I'll ask him."

"Mom knows more," Cyril said quietly.

Rose nodded and said, "Your dad worked in the mines that dug up coal for the railways."

"Yeah," Cyril added. "Big engines that blew out lots of smoke and pulled long lines of cars. Some with people in them. I remember that."

"Then why did we leave?" Amelia asked, frowning.

"The mine closed," Rose said. "There was only so much coal they could dig out that was of any value."

It was starting to get dark. Cyril might have added more from his shadowy childhood memories. He also had a big secret simmering just below the surface.

If Rose had been able to see him clearly in the dim light, she might have asked him what he was thinking. Or maybe not. There were too many secrets and too many things unspoken in their Athabasca solitude, so far away from previous memories.

There were too many secrets stifled by the demands of survival and the labor it imposed.

Two, maybe three days later, Rose began to worry. Jack should have been back if everything had gone well. Even if Mr. Harley and his canoe full of pelts hadn't been at the meeting place, Jack would have been sent home. Malcolm would have sent him back, as in previous years. It would only have taken him a day. Less, if the current was strong, and Jack had been able to take advantage of it. Rose knew that, too.

"Jack should be home this evening at the latest," Rose said to no one in particular.

"We could go down and wait for him, couldn't we, Mom?" Amelia asked. "And Cyril could do some fishing."

"Nothing's biting now. The fish aren't moving anywhere." Cyril said it with finality. There was an edge to his voice.

Rose took that as a sign of Cyril's own anxiety. Jack was Cyril's only companion. They were all each of them had out here. They were boys. They did boy things, as Rose imagined it. So, like her, Cyril was right to be worried.

But Amelia wasn't. She was in Rose's image, and her helper.

As the three of them headed out, anxious to find out something, Amelia skipped on ahead on the trail to the river.

The three of them watched the river flow by near the shore,

and then looked to the farthest point beyond the bend. They could hear the river hiss over nearby gravel bars and gurgle in the eddying currents farther out. Even the small canoe would have been able to cover a hundred miles, traveling downstream, if it stayed in the stronger currents.

"How far is it to where they meet up with Mr. Harley?" Rose asked, looking over at Cyril.

"Seventy miles, I think Jack told me," Cyril answered.

Finally, as darkness seeped into the Athabasca valley, and only the peaks of some of the visible foothills still reached up into the sunlight, Rose said, "Jack will be pulled out and camped somewhere by now. He knows not to risk the river in the dark, no matter how close to home he is."

She nodded for Cyril and Amelia to start back up to the house, while she scanned the river one more time. Not knowing was always the hardest.

Maybe it was because of that, of seeing the worry in his mom's face, as they later sat in the glow of the coal oil lamp, that Cyril let the words fall out of his mouth.

"He's not coming back."

"What?"

"He told me not to tell you. But Jack's not coming back." And with that statement, and all its implications, Cyril began to sob uncontrollably. It was a throbbing explosion of fear, anger, grief, remorse, and the deepening agony of not knowing exactly where his brother was.

As Amelia whimpered in the background, Cyril finally sobbed, "He told me not to tell. He told me to wait at least a week. He said he was old enough to be out on his own."

Even in the light of the lamp, it was as if a dark cloud had settled over them. A cloud that had always been there, like some foreboding omen, but which now could not be held back any longer. It was like some inevitable tragedy had deepened the misery of their lives. Logically, Rose might have anticipated that some unforeseen disaster would sooner or later overtake them in their isolation. She might have anticipated some force of nature—something beyond their control. But this was personal, and deeply painful.

"Jack said he wouldn't be able to stay through the next winter," Cyril said. Then he added, "He knew he wouldn't be able to go out on the trap lines with Dad."

Cyril might have added more, but he'd glanced over at Amelia.

Rose nodded. "I know," she said softly. "I've had my fears."

7

"Show me where," Rose said with quiet authority the next morning, looking over at Cyril. "Show me where Jack made a cache of supplies for his trip."

"He never showed me," Cyril answered, understanding the question and realizing the implications. "All he said was that he'd keep some secrets to himself. Maybe he didn't trust me."

"Yes, that would have been a heavy load for you to bear," Rose told him, nodding slowly. "Especially with what you already knew."

"He just said he'd store some stuff downstream, maybe near a special tree or other marker." Cyril remembered their conversation from the night before they'd loaded up the furs. He remembered thinking it strange that Jack had said even that much. Especially when he didn't really need to.

"We'll go and look after lunch," Rose told Cyril and Amelia. But then, almost as soon as she'd said it, she said, "No, we'll go and look now." She led the way down to the river, almost at a run.

Rose waded out into the Athabasca to look up into the bordering forests. She searched for any tree that might stand out as a marker, like Cyril had mentioned. But she saw nothing. No large ancient pine that might have been overlooked by lumbermen in earlier years.

"It wouldn't be this close to the trail," Cyril suggested, as he walked along the shore, trying to come to a spot below where Jack's lookout was.

"That's it!" Rose said. "That's it, isn't it?" she repeated, looking over at Cyril for confirmation when she spotted a big pine tree.

Cyril nodded. He could see where the brush had recently been pushed aside. Jack had been there, possibly on his return trip from the Hinton run.

Rose forged into the bush and looked up at the same time, trying to keep sight of the big pine. But there was nothing at the base of the tree. No hollow or anything like that. Of course not. Jack would have taken as little as possible to hide down here for his trip, so as not to attract attention. Rose knew that. Anything removed from her stores would have been noticed. Jack would have done it over a few weeks to avoid suspicion.

"Mom!" Amelia had kept walking and looking up. "Mom! There's a red cloth of some sort."

Just barely visible, in the first crook of a sapling, Jack had wedged a small medicine bottle and used a tag of red cloth as a stopper.

"Like a message in a bottle," Amelia whispered, as Rose pulled the bottle from its perch. Her hands were shaking, as she pulled out the red plug and then shook out a small, rolled-up piece of paper. She wondered when and where Jack must have written it. How long had he been committed to this desperate undertaking?

Rose's hand trembled and she had to wipe at her eyes, as she quietly mouthed the words of her son's note.

Mom, I had to do this. You know I did. And you know I couldn't tell you. I had to do this myself or there would have been trouble for anyone I told. And you would have tried to stop me. It is like some of the stories in our reading books that you taught us. I have to go and find myself. The young eagles do this every year. It is not easy for them. But I have watched them, and they always seem to do all right. I cannot say where I am going because I do not know yet. Mr. Harley last year talked some about the fur trading days, when people traveled up and down this river. I have matches and that small ax that Dad thought he had lost trapping. I did not take much food because it is summer.

Thanks for being my mom. I will come back. Jack.

"He'll be back when he's ready. He's all right. He knows how to use that little canoe."

Rose said these things slowly, not looking at either Cyril or Amelia. Saying them out loud so that it might make them true. She dabbed at her eyes and then at her nose, as she led them back up to the house. If she had looked up into the midday sky, she would have seen a couple of Jack's eagles circling up on the rising currents of air.

"But that little canoe is Dad's trapping canoe," Amelia said, as they stepped out of the bush near their little log house. "How will Dad go up the little river to scout out the beaver dams and take supplies up to his cabin?"

That was the way it had always been. In the fall, Malcolm Whyte had always ferried things up to his trapping cabin, and made sure things were in order for the winter. The small canoe had been his way to do that.

"Fall's a long way off, Amelia. A lot can happen in the meantime," Cyril told her.

Rose heard him and nodded to herself. But, as a mother, she dared not give voice to her dread and foreboding.

8

Jack had only ever looked forward to the spring trip for one reason. That was when they would meet up with Mr. Harley, their only nearby contact—if he could be called that—with the outside world.

The Whyte children had always only referred to him as Mr. Harley. Perhaps it was a sign of politeness, in which Rose had encouraged them, or maybe he was important as their only neighbor, and probably the only one who knew that the Whyte family existed, and where they lived.

Harley was already at the junction of a creek, where there was a flat place to camp for the night. The creek was slow and sluggish and afforded Malcolm a place to tie up his big canoe without unloading it. The smaller canoe would be whatever shelter he and Jack might need for the night.

"Good winter?" Malcolm asked Harley, who hadn't risen from beside his fire.

"Ah, you know." Harley let the words hiss out quietly between his teeth. "You?"

"About the same, I guess."

It would take a while for either of the men to get into the rhythm of talking again. The long winter may have thawed with the spring, but the warmth of a new summer had not yet had the same effect on their tongues.

Not that either of them lived alone. Malcolm had his family, and Harley, as he had revealed at their second meeting, had a wife of sorts. She was an Indian woman who, apparently, was a match for his taciturn ways, and who expected little in return for the work she did in their house or camp, somewhere up toward the foothills.

Maybe it worked for them because Harley was a Métis, who had followed the rivers out this way from the Battle River, when too much progress from the railways had pushed him toward the solitude of the mountains. Harley never mentioned his woman's name. He just kind of chuckled one time, saying she could skin a rabbit faster and better than he could.

Jack earned his spot by the fire with the men by bringing in enough firewood for the night. Not a hard thing to do now that the river had receded from its spring flood, leaving a lot of driftwood up at its high-water mark. He'd noticed a couple of fish, gutted, splayed, and propped to cook by the fire. He also saw other things, aside from the fish, that indicated that Harley had been camped there for at least a day or so.

Malcolm nodded toward his son. "Tea, Jack."

It was the signal for Jack to fetch some clear water and set the tin in the coals of the fire. The tea would get maybe a second or third boiling before the evening was over, if there was enough to talk about.

"There must be lots of berries up where you are," Malcolm said, when Harley brought a small bag of what he called sausage over to the fire, after the sun had set.

In the old days, it might have been called pemmican. It was stuff that Harley's woman had pounded together, made of dried meat, animal fat, and dried berries. She'd squeezed it all into long sleeves of cloth, and then smoked them slowly beside a fire. The smoke cured and dried it some more, and had the added benefit of giving it a salty flavor.

"Drink tea," Harley suggested, or warned, as Jack began chewing on his second mouthful. "Don't eat too much at once." He left it at that, knowing that Jack would learn soon enough on his own.

"I wonder what the railways are up to these days?" Malcolm floated the question over the fire, as a way of giving Harley a chance to speak about the news he might know.

"They move faster and faster, those things," Harley muttered.

"They've been working on a rail line to go north. It crosses somewhere downstream." He didn't sound happy to say it.

Malcolm nodded, waiting for more.

Jack said nothing either, but he wondered about what might be happening downstream, and where that might be.

"Change, change," Harley hissed.

Jack didn't look over at him, out of politeness or deference, but he could imagine Mr. Harley shaking his head as he said it.

"First the traders, then the farmers and the lumbermen. And then the railways to make it all go faster." Harley shook his head.

"It makes you wonder what's next, doesn't it?" Malcolm prompted. Although Jack couldn't understand why. He'd seldom heard his father talk so much, or for so long.

"They will find something," Harley said. "Just like they found the farmland up by the Peace River. They want to put plows and farms up there, where things to eat won't even grow."

At that point, Jack didn't know whether Mr. Harley was growling, or maybe just quietly laughing. He didn't look over to find out. He just kept on listening, and thinking, and wondering.

"Soon the prairies and the bush will all disappear, like the buffalo and the beaver."

They might have talked some more, but Jack didn't find out. His dad nodded for him to crawl in under the canoe for the night. He was probably ready. He'd been in the water, pulling the canoes for most of the day. And most of that up to his waist and beyond in the cold Athabasca.

Jack would have liked to hear more, but tomorrow he would be on his own. He had a lot to think about.

Jack wondered about his big decision, as he rolled himself up into his blanket, somewhat sheltered by their small canoe. It was old and beat up, with lots of patches on its canvas. Most of them were just tarred into place. He wondered how the canoe would stand up to the trip that he intended to take. He also wondered about Cyril, the only one who knew something of his plans. Then he wondered about the three of them—Cyril, Amelia, and his mom—waiting at the house, downstream. Waiting and wondering, too, he imagined.

Jack pretended to be asleep when Malcolm finally turned in for the night, banging his head on the gunwale as he did so. Jack tried to focus on the stars moving above them. Eventually he did fall asleep. Tiredness had overcome doubt and worry.

9

"Now, boy."

It was the next thing Jack heard. And with that command, Malcolm nudged his son's feet.

Malcolm was already standing in the still dark mist that wafted around them. The hiss of the river's currents and eddies was the only noise. That and the snapping of twigs, as Harley blew the coals of their fire back to life, and then encouraged the flames with larger and larger kindling, and then branches of driftwood that Jack had laid by the evening before.

There was time for tea and a bite of the sausage that Harley offered again. Then Jack watched, as Harley and his dad tossed their things into their canoes, checked the lashing of things, and then climbed in themselves. Jack had only served to speed things up for his dad until they got to this point. From here, Malcolm and Harley would help each other around or through any hard spots. Jack had learned in his first year of helping that his dad did not want his company up to Hinton. He'd known better than to ask why, even back then.

Jack kicked the fire apart as a precaution, even though there wasn't much left but coals. He then looked around at the world of the river that was now all his own. He tied his blanket pack and spare paddle to the center thwart in the canoe, and set it into the pool of the small creek from which his dad and Mr. Harley had set out a while before. He had no other gear and no food. He knew his dad would not want him to have any excuse or reason to dawdle.

The small canoe and the river's currents had been the only sport that Jack and Cyril had known in their summers beside the Athabasca. Close to their house, the river was slow enough for them to experiment and learn what it took to make the little canoe do what they wanted it to. Malcolm had been down there to guide them at first. Probably because Rose had insisted or threatened in some fashion. Jack later suspected that his dad had been concerned for the safety of his work canoe.

"Well, here we go," Jack whispered to the small canoe, as he rested on both gunwales and climbed aboard.

With a few strokes, Jack was into the current of the Athabasca. He had done this trip, and helped with the furs in the large canoe, three times before. Depending on the currents, it usually took five or six days of hard work to cover the seventy miles upstream, and then one day for the trip back down. He'd always been told to pull out an hour before dark, if it took longer.

The wind was from the south, funneling along the river valley. A good day to be letting it help push him along. The added push gave Jack the opportunity to look around. He was surprised at how much he remembered from previous trips. At least the trips downstream, going back. Going upstream, to link up with Mr. Harley, there had been too much work, just to keep the big canoe moving.

But now, easing along in the sunshine, Jack had time to look and think. He could see elk along the shores from time to time, as well as other smaller game. There were also a few eagles taking advantage of the south wind.

The darker the water, the faster it moved. Dark water was where the deep channels were, and the faster currents. The noisy, frothy stuff elsewhere indicated the places where the river was shallow, or maybe a stretch of rapids.

At one point, Jack said, "Damn!" quietly to himself. He had been dreaming or thinking, and hadn't heard the gravel starting to tumble and bounce under the bottom of his canoe before it was too late, and he had to step out and float the canoe over a gravel bar in the middle of the river. He could imagine the eagles up above, laughing.

The river was never the same, even from day to day. Its level fluctuated with the seasons, and pulsed in harmony with the storms and rains up higher in the mountain valleys, right up to the glaciers. Jack remembered Mr. Harley once saying that the heart of the river was up in the high mountains. That had been a couple of years ago, when they had waited out a storm at the meeting place.

The sun was about an hour above the trees, when Jack came to a bend and a small island that he recognized as the last one before he got close to home. There would not be enough time to pick up his things where he had stored them and get a good distance farther down the river. He decided to pull out on the eastern shore and spend the night. That way he could also look over to where their house was, and maybe see some signs of activity. Maybe some smoke rising up when his mom would be cooking.

Jack thought of building a fire for himself, but soon put that out of his mind. If he could maybe see the smoke from the house, then they might see the smoke in the river valley. He knew, or imagined, they would be looking for him—although he knew it wasn't too unusual for other people to be traveling up or down the river sometimes.

He and Cyril had often wondered about what it might have been like when the Athabasca River was one of the east-west trade routes, back in the really old days. That was when Jasper House had been an outpost, and when Fort Assiniboine had been the terminus for the overland route to Edmonton and its fort on the North Saskatchewan River. But, for more than fifty years now, it had been the railways that had taken on the role of linking east and west, and branching out to bring in many more resources than the rivers ever had.

Jack shivered through the night. And then, in the gray light of dawn, he listened for any echoing sounds of an ax that might tell him someone was awake across the river. Finally, he wished for a wind to blow the mists away, so he could cross over and cover the last few hundred yards to where he had cached his supplies.

"I hope my things are there," Jack whispered to himself, knowing that if they weren't, Cyril had not kept his secret. And yet, he almost wished they might not be. He had planned all of this for more than a year. But now, now that it was time to actually do it, he almost wished he didn't have to go through with it.

Jack spotted the ancient pine standing out from the rest of the forest, as he eased his way down the river, and then waded his little canoe ashore. His small stash of supplies was wrapped in oilcloth near the base of the pine. It was as he had left it. That, and the little canoe were his passport to a new life.

He ached as he took the little bottle with the note from the folds of the oilcloth and placed it in the crook of a sapling near the pine. A piece of red cloth acted as its stopper. Tears welled in his eyes, as he remembered what he had written. He blinked and imagined how it might be read. He'd told Cyril he would leave a note. It was the only way. Jack knew he would not be able to face his mom and explain his decision. He knew she would have many arguments and reasons for him not to go through with it.

It was about midday when Jack glided onto the upper end of a small island. He wanted to be able to look back as far as possible, even though he knew no one would be able to come after him. The big canoe would still be within a day or so of reaching Hinton, and he had the only other canoe. Maybe he just wanted to take one last look up into the valley that had been his home for more than half his lifetime. Maybe he needed to think and reassure himself.

"Maybe what I really need to do is eat."

Jack said it out loud to fill the emptiness, and was actually startled to realize just how loud his voice could be in the wilderness, with nothing but the steady hiss of the river to mute it.

Jack pulled out a couple of small rubbery potatoes he had taken from the root cellar. Seed potatoes, maybe. He'd wondered at the time if his mom would notice. He rubbed off the eyes and washed them in the cold water of the Athabasca. He munched slowly on small bites of potato, figuring that the slower he ate, the more his hunger could be controlled.

"It's the only way, isn't it?" Jack reasoned within himself. "I'll sort things out at Whitecourt. Maybe I'll even get a job there." Then he wondered how a person went about becoming a lumberman, or maybe hiring on with a farm. Really, he didn't know how many, or how few, his possibilities were.

He savored the last mouthful of his second little potato, rolled up his oilcloth and his supplies, and set off again.

Jack paddled and drifted as long as he could, before calling it a day. He'd frequently caught himself looking back over his shoulder. Finally, he pulled in at the mouth of a small creek on the western shore, thinking it would be good to wake up on the sunny side of the river. He also hoped he could get a fish in the creek. He knew it was too early for berries of any kind.

It didn't take him long to organize a fire and touch one of his matches to the shavings and the kindling. With a fire going, he lifted the canoe up to a flat spot, pulled out his supplies, and set his tin to boiling in the edge of the fire. Two of his dozen carrots from the root cellar would be his supper. That and whatever else he might find close at hand. Fish, maybe, if he was lucky and patient.

Maybe a half-hour later, not fish, but frog legs went into the pot.

Hunger and the vagaries of nature can impose some odd compromises on a person's meal. Jack mused about such things as he dumped the severed hindquarters of three frogs into the pot to join the simmering chunks of carrot.

Actually, it wasn't entirely a novelty. Jack could remember

when he and Cyril had made some boyhood experiments with frogs and other small "game," as they had called them in their previous summer adventures. It did make his tea taste a bit oily, though, when he boiled some up later in the evening.

When the sun settled into the mountains behind him, the campfire became Jack's friend and muse. Had he reached the point of no return?

No, that had probably come during the last winter. That was the night when, under a full moon, Jack had been helping his dad stretch some pelts harvested from a small trap line close to the house. And, of course, he hadn't done it right, or hadn't done it the way his dad had wanted. But then, had he ever been able to please his dad in anything?

Whatever the problem or argument had been, Jack remembered facing up to his dad and squaring off. Even if he could not remember the argument, he could remember standing there, looking straight back at his father, and thinking it would not be much longer before he'd be as tall as him.

But what really stood out in his memory, when he'd set back to work at his father's orders, was that he had had his hand clenched around the small skinning knife. And, when he looked down, he could not tell where the blood from the mink ended and his own began. He also knew that some future confrontation would not, or could not, end with one of them backing down.

Jack also realized he did not understand his father. Probably never would. Maybe they were too much alike in their stubbornness.

In the enervating midday heat of the next day, Jack said a quiet, "Oh-oh," as he looked farther ahead than the immediate current. On one side of the river, there were steep bluffs denuded of trees, and a lot more large boulders then there had been upstream. And the river itself seemed to drop away. Safety dictated that he should land, walk ahead along the shore, and see what might be in store for him and his little canoe.

Jack was suddenly out of his afternoon doldrums and alert to his surroundings. He knew he had to land his canoe on the inside of the coming bend and its possibly rough water. It was only by getting out and wading that he was able to pull his canoe to shore in a current that now seemed to be slipping sideways.

It was a beautiful summer day. If it had been him and Cyril out on a day's adventure, they would have laughed at the challenge ahead. They would also have taken it as a sign to explore for a while, and then head back. But this was the first big challenge of Jack's new life. One that he would have to deal with on his own.

Jack knew the first rule that safety imposed—check what's ahead.

He imagined a narrowing channel through a gorge, with white water at its base. As he picked his way over boulders and gravel bars, and the inevitable tangles of uprooted trees and driftwood that had been washed down from somewhere during a spring break-up, Jack had a religious expletive to add to his earlier, "Oh-oh." An entirely logical "Holy shit!" was offered in reverent and solemn respect for the might of the Athabasca River, at this point in its descent.

Jack had heard of something called the Gooseneck rapids. Probably from Mr. Harley at an evening cooking fire one year. He'd described the river as splitting and forging its way around an island in a long, sweeping bend.

"That must be the Gooseneck," Jack whispered to himself, as he surveyed the reality of what Mr. Harley had described. "And that's the neck of the beast," Jack said at last. "That's the side to avoid."

However, avoiding it, and getting to the smaller channel on the inner side of the island, presented a challenge. And that channel, the one Mr. Harley had said the fur traders called "the voyageur channel," was one whose approach, or entrance, he had sailed right by, while mesmerized by the tumbling waters of the main channel.

"Shit!" Jack yelled in frustration and anger. Frustration at having come upon such an enormous obstacle. Anger at having come this far and now having to look for an alternative. Something that obviously wouldn't be easy to do.

When you're caught, or trapped, you look around. First at the enemy, then at the situation, and then at a possible escape or alternative. All of it made Jack say, "Shit!" again. Several times. He even shouted it the last time, just because he could. He was alone. He was boss. He was in charge and responsible for his own destiny. And he had made a mistake!

"Damn it all!"

As he looked around, he wasn't even sure that the one dark shadow he had passed was the voyageur channel. It was just a hole, sheltered by some overhanging trees on one side, and some rocky outcroppings jutting out into the river on the other. He'd have to fight his way back up to those rocks, just to be sure. Going upstream, at least, was one thing with which he was more than a bit familiar.

It didn't take Jack long to drag the small canoe back to that rocky point to check things out. His frustration soon turned to smiles, as he bounded along on the island side of a small channel and discovered that he was, indeed, on an island, and looking at a route that would avoid the Gooseneck rapids in a series of gradual steps.

Jack checked his little canoe and the few things he had brought with him. He made sure things were lashed in, as he realized that, once again, he had come to a point of no return. At least, not an easy one.

Often, when you've selected the most agreeable of two options, you let your guard down, just a bit. Maybe because you think that success is within your grasp. This is not a lesson that can be taught. It is learned through experience.

Jack didn't say "oh-oh" again until he got close to the end of the voyageur channel—the last step before it merged with the main river again.

Here, the smaller channel slid sideways in a long bend along the Athabasca shore. It was a bend that was overhung with trees, toppled in the spring run-off. Jack and his canoe were swept toward that shore.

There was no way out. No way to dig in and keep the canoe from getting sucked along in the current at the outside of that bend.

Only in hindsight did Jack recall the instant that lasted for an eternity, in which he was swatted out of the canoe by the prickly branches of a teetering spruce, while the canoe ran into a submerged boulder that forced it broadside to the current, swamping it.

In that same instant, he remembered that the canoe was his only lifeline in those rapids, and his only means of escape to a new life. All he could do was react, reach out, grab for some part of the canoe, and hang on. It's only afterward, if you survive, that you realize what you really should have done. But in that instant, gasping for air, being twisted about, and impelled onward by the unrelenting hydraulic power of the river, Jack clung to what he could and tried to save himself and his canoe.

Jack was fifteen. He weighed maybe a hundred and twenty pounds. As it capsized and rolled and tumbled in the current, his little canoe had the weight and strength of ten men. The canoe fell victim to the current, and Jack fell victim to the canoe. He hung on in desperation. He also knew that, in one of those twists and tumbles, something in his left arm had not been strong enough.

Maybe it was the coldness of the water. Maybe it was the terror of the instant. Maybe it was his own anger and rebellious temper. Whatever it was, Jack felt little or no pain until, at the end of the rapids, the river leveled, and he managed to kick himself and his canoe out of the strength of the current and into the shelter of a backwater. With his right arm, he dragged the canoe slowly up and through the silt of a gravel bar, taking care to let the water drain out slowly as he did so, to prevent any further damage to the canoe. Finally, he slowly rolled it to release the water that was left, beached it, and then collapsed onto the sunny warmth of the bar itself.

A throbbing pain in his left arm roused him. A sharp, biting pain that made Jack wince and brought tears to his eyes. He knew something was broken. His escape had come to an end.

Jack sat up slowly, cradling his left arm, and tried to figure out exactly where the pain was coming from. His fingers tingled. His shoulder was sore and stiff, although he realized the stiffness might be from trying to hold his arm still and motionless, to ease the stabbing of the pain. For how long, he didn't know. He looked down at the sleeve on his forearm, and wondered how much it might hurt if he were to roll it back. He wondered and feared what he might see.

Nothing! After slowly edging his cuff back to his elbow, all Jack could see, just below his elbow, was the beginning of a bruise. "Maybe," he thought, "maybe that's all it is."

He'd seen the bones of animals maimed in traps. Bones that had snapped and then jutted up through the skin. Jack remembered feeling, or sensing, something snap. Gingerly he touched the bruising. Slowly he tried to rotate his wrist. And instantly he knew that his first fear had been correct.

It was probably late or mid afternoon. The sun was drying his clothes, as he sat on the gravel shore at the edge of the river and tried to think. Jack looked at his canoe and was relieved to see that his oilcloth bundle was still lashed to the center thwart, and that the spare paddle was still lashed beside it. That much, at least, he had managed to do correctly.

Jack also noticed the river. He was surprised to see, from where he sat, that it looked almost calm and benign. Only when he looked upstream could he see the telltale glistening of cresting waves, or stacks, that indicated rapids and a current that was faster than any canoe, whatever its size, or how it was manned.

"I guess I'll have to stay put for a while," Jack told himself. He said it out loud just to be sure he understood that it might be a while before some healing in his left arm would let him paddle again, and continue the journey to his new life. He surveyed his surroundings and realized, once again, that nature was in charge.

"But not entirely," Jack reminded himself. Or maybe it was the message of hunger rumbling up from his stomach. "I've still got to look after myself."

He looked along the shore behind him for a suitable place to hole up. For how long, he didn't know. But as soon as he moved even a little, he realized he would not be leaving for a few days. Maybe weeks. He tried to remember, if ever he had known, just how long it took for bones to mend. He also knew, when he moved again, that he'd have to do something to keep his arm immobile.

As he continued to sit and look around and take stock, Jack realized that the Athabasca now seemed to be flowing eastward. No matter where he camped on this shore, he'd probably see the sun rise and the sun set.

It was the last thing he remembered with any certainty for a long while, as the pain began to dominate whatever he did, or tried to do.

10

Malcolm Whyte was in a surprisingly good mood, as he maneuvered his big canoe out of the stronger current, and headed for the shore below his house in the Athabasca forest lands, in the foothills of the Rocky Mountains. His mood was the result of getting more for his furs than he had anticipated, and the subsequent ability to purchase all the things on his, or Rose's, long list, as well as a few bonus items. He even anticipated that they might actually celebrate Christmas in the coming winter.

It was with a fair amount of exuberance that Malcolm pulled up, secured his canoe, lifted one special pack out of it, and headed up to the house. He anticipated the competition among the eager hands of his family to carry up the rest, when they realized he was home already. He was even glad they weren't waiting down by the river, as they had at other times. Or, at least Cyril, acting as a lookout. But he had pushed himself to make it home that day, when sunset already threatened.

What Malcolm had not expected was the cloud of silence when he came through the door. A cloud that could only mean a disaster or tragedy of some sort. He looked from one to the other, trying to imagine what it might be.

"Jack's gone," Amelia whispered in response to her father's questioning look.

"He's fifteen. He thought it was time," Cyril added, trying to explain.

Malcolm might have anticipated it, but he had not expected it. Not yet. Not this way. He also knew this was not the petulance and running away of a child, whose adventure would end by the time smoke from the supper cook stove curled up through the chimney.

Without looking up, Malcolm handed Rose the pack he had carried up. "This is for you," he said. "It wasn't on the list." Then, avoiding her eyes, he told them all, "There's a canoe full of supplies to haul up to the house before it gets too dark. After that, we'll talk."

Malcolm Whyte was in charge. But, in that brief exchange, he realized he had never been less in charge. He felt like the commander of an army that had deserted him. Everything that this wilderness homestead was supposed to be had changed. Everything in the canoe, waiting to be unloaded, was diminished.

The sun had set by the time Cyril had helped his dad pull

the canoe up into the bush, tied it down, and the last bundle had been brought up to the house. Unpacking and sorting could wait.

Malcolm lit the coal oil lamp and asked, "Where did he go, and why?" Although he knew as soon as he said it, that he should not have asked the second part of that question.

That question triggered the release of all the years of emotion that had been set aside, hidden, or ignored, among all the other priorities of just trying to survive in the wilderness for the last seven years.

"Why?" Rose almost spat out the word, drawing it out like it was the biggest and most formidable in her vocabulary. "Why?"

When she repeated it, Malcolm motioned Cyril and Amelia over to the door.

"No!" Rose yelled, moving to cut off their escape. "They are a part of this, too. They may even have something to say. We've all been silent for far too long."

Cyril and Amelia moved out of the orange glow of the lamp and stood like dim shadows of themselves. Visible, but out of the line of fire. This, like the events of the days before, would be seared into their memories.

"Jack's got the small canoe," Rose stated. "He's gone upriver, or down. But if you didn't see him, then I guess he's gone downriver." She breathed deeply, and more quietly added, "He left a note. It didn't say much."

Avoiding the formidable question of why, Malcolm looked over into the shadows and asked Cyril, "Do you know where?"

Cyril shook his head.

"Where?" Rose spat out the word. "The Athabasca goes to all the rest of Canada, and everything beyond that! Didn't you and the Whitecourt boys discover that when you went off to fight in the war?"

Malcolm nodded vaguely. He knew that to say anything more would only make things worse. He needed to think. He needed to retreat. He needed to let the dust and debris of the explosion settle down.

And that was what he said as he opened the door. "I need to think. I'll be out in the shed."

Cyril and Amelia had heard their father's outbursts before. And they had heard the silence. They had not yet figured out which of the two was the most intimidating or alarming.

"Are we all right, Mom?" Cyril asked after a while.

When Amelia continued to whimper and sniffle, Rose replied, "Yes, we're all right."

Rose blew out the candle before the three of them went to bed. She knew Malcolm would be watching from somewhere. She also knew that none of them, wherever they were, would get much sleep that night.

11

"I'll bring him home," was all Malcolm said, as he opened the door to the house in the morning, and just as quietly shut it again.

With only the light load of Malcolm's trapping and hunting pack, always at the ready, the big canoe was harder to handle in the wind and currents of the Athabasca and its meandering valley. With the big load coming down from Hinton, it had been stable and steady, and relatively easy for one man to keep in the propelling currents. But without a load, it bounded along and danced in the currents.

Malcolm knew Jack might consider Whitecourt. It was a small village, with a post office and a general store, central to the pioneers who had settled in that area. But then he reasoned that Jack would probably not stay there, since it was the first place downstream and easy to get to. He wondered how angry and rebellious Jack would have to be to keep ahead of him, and how clever, in order not to leave any sign of his traveling downstream.

Malcolm muttered to himself when, late in the afternoon, he came to an island he remembered from years before, and whose features were the inspiration for local legends and tales. The sweeping bend around the island created rapids that only a fool would attempt by himself, and which had swamped even experienced crews in larger canoes.

He looked at the descending sun, and realized he would have to spend a night above the island, and its nearly hidden voyageur channel. He'd have to check the route and then descend in the morning. He found a suitable place to land and camp for the night.

Sitting beside his campfire, sipping his first boil of tea, Malcolm tried to think back to when he had been fifteen. It was not an easy task. Maybe because he had spent too much time trying to forget too many things from his earlier life. It would be another long night.

A strong and early wind the next morning blew the swirling river mists upstream. Malcolm made no morning fire. His work with the canoe would warm him soon enough. He looked for and trimmed off a sturdy sapling to use as a pole in the rapids, should he need it. The pole lay ready and within reach. It would be a brake when necessary.

There was no rush to get through and beyond the island, to where the river would level off for a while to a more manageable speed. Going slowly let him guide the canoe with his pole, while the current provided propulsion. Malcolm stayed in the shallow water close to the island. When he saw the main river again, he dug in hard, and slowly let the canoe slide down to the next level, without getting swept to the outside of the bend with its overhanging trees. Gravel and stones rattled against the bottom of the canoe in the frothy shallows.

At last, Malcolm felt his canoe settle into a backwater at the bottom end of the island. He looked over to where the standing waves of the Gooseneck rapids marked the bottom end of that dangerous obstacle. He was past and beyond. He switched back to his paddle, as he looked around at the power of the river. And he looked for any signs that his son had passed through there. Although, if he had seen anything, it would indicate the worst possible outcome. For that reason, Malcolm was relieved, as he pulled for the current to resume his descent on the Athabasca in search of his canoe, and his son.

Or not. He had hardly rejoined the stream, when he noticed the shape of a canoe on the shaded, southern shore of the river. It was rolled over onto its side, but not very far up. Hardly a desirable campsite.

It didn't take Malcolm long to realize that he had caught up with Jack. He also knew something must be wrong. The only positive sign was a huddled form near the canoe, sitting sort of upright.

12

Jack had noticed the canoe in the river. He'd noticed and recognized it. Oddly, his thoughts went to winter, and scenes of animals caught in traps. Caught, but not killed. Caught, and not knowing what to expect next. Caught, and not knowing anything except that there was no escape.

"How long have you been here?" Malcolm asked with uncustomary quiet control.

"A few days, I think."

"Why?"

"My arm broke." Jack said it with certainty and finality. He was ashen and cold.

The sun was finally high enough to bring sunshine and warmth to the shore where Jack was sitting. He had been waiting for that. Waiting and knowing that when the sun warmed him enough, he might test his arm again and try to do something. Maybe figure out a way to keep it still and ease the pain.

Malcolm did not wait. He brought his canvas pack, set it near the smaller canoe, and set about building a fire on the downwind side of the boy.

Within a half-hour, Malcolm had boiled up some tea, poured some into an old enameled cup, sweetened it with the thick Eagle Brand condensed milk from one of several small tins he usually carried with him, and held it out to the boy.

"Drink it, son." It was the first compassionate thing he'd said since landing. It was not a tone with which Jack was familiar.

Jack looked up, wondering if he'd heard right. Maybe it was the numbness of another long night, the cold, and the pain. He hadn't ever broken anything before. He didn't know how it would affect him. He wondered about all of that, as his right hand received the cup. It was shaking. He feared he might spill the tea.

The sweetness and warmth of the tea was medicinal in its affect. Jack sipped its heat, and then he drank it down as it became cool enough. Then he watched, as the man who had called him "son" set some fresh water in the edge of the fire, and began cutting into it the carrots and the two small potatoes still in his oilcloth pack. It took on the qualities of a stew or soup when he cut up some fire-dried meat, or jerky, into it.

Jack just sat and watched. He tried to think, as the warmth of the sun and the tea seeped through him. He also began to wonder what would happen next. He wondered if he should feel captured or rescued. Or, more to the point, he wondered how his dad would eventually react to all of this. What had his dad expected to find, anyway? Had he even expected to catch up to him, or just to go as far as Whitecourt, to find out where he might have gone? Would he even have gone as far as Whitecourt?

Malcolm had gathered more firewood. Probably to keep busy and to do something. He'd also checked on the soupy stew bubbling by the fire.

After a while, he took the enameled cup from Jack, rinsed it in the river, and dipped it into the tin. The aroma made Jack realize he was very hungry.

"We'll have to look at that arm," Malcolm said, after Jack had blown over the soup to cool it and tested its contents. "That arm will let us know what we can do next."

Jack nodded. He hadn't looked at it since that first time. He'd been afraid of what he might see. He knew it would hurt. He was still afraid, because he knew it would dictate any decisions he might still be able to make. He also watched his dad, who had found a piece of cedar and, with some deft strokes of his big knife, whittled a spoon to dig into what was left in the cooking tin. Jack knew his dad never carried a spoon with him. Complained that utensils got lost. "But," Jack remembered him saying, "there's always wood to carve into whatever you need." He never explained how he always managed to hang onto his knife.

The fire was reduced to coals. The heat of the sun was more than enough for warmth. Malcolm rinsed out the cooking tin and set it, half full, in the coals for more tea.

"We need to use what's left in that little tin of milk," he said by way of explanation. Or maybe he said it to fill the void between them.

"The soup was good," Jack said. "Moose?" he asked, wondering about the meat, or jerky.

Malcolm nodded vaguely. Then after a while, he said, "When you're ready," looking at Jack's arm.

"All right," Jack said, and winced as he turned toward his dad. He realized the tea that was just starting to simmer was intended to alleviate whatever might come next. He hoped it would be strong, and that there was still a lot of that sweet, thick milk to add to it.

"You know that it's broken?" Malcolm asked, as Jack slowly pulled the sleeve of his shirt back.

Jack nodded, clenched his teeth, and wheezed, "I felt something snap."

There was a large, bluish-gray area on his forearm. From his elbow down, his arm and wrist felt numb.

Jack grimaced when he tried to move his fingers. The color vanished from his features.

Jack's look and reaction were not unfamiliar to Malcolm. He'd been through a war twenty years before. There had been guns and armaments, and many reasons for men to be hurt or killed. There had been shouts of men trying to bring order out of that chaos. All of that, and the cries of indescribable pain.

"Hold still, boy. You'll be all right. That arm will heal. But we need to get it immobilized."

With his arm resting on his lap, Jack could feel its pain absorb the warmth of the afternoon sun. He looked up to respond to his dad, to say that he was all right, that he would manage once he'd rested. But his dad was gone.

Jack turned to look, but the pain brought him back to facing the river as before. He looked down at his arm again and wondered what had happened. He felt like he had disappeared. Then he noticed the cup beside him, full of tea, and almost white with the sweet milk. He wondered how, or why, or what had happened to make things go blank and the world disappear.

Malcolm was back before Jack had finished the tea. He was carrying a scroll of birch bark.

"We'll wrap this around your arm to keep it immobile," he said. "Like a splint."

Jack wondered if he might disappear into the pain again, as his dad began to work. But he was surprised at how firm and gentle the man could be, as he first padded his arm with a patch of blanket, and then fashioned the birch bark around it like a tube. All of his left arm, right down to the fingertips, he tied with strips he tore from the oilcloth.

Jack hoped his dad hadn't seen him looking at him, as he knelt beside him and worked on his arm in silence. It was not something he had ever dared to do before, that he could remember. Not up that close.

"We'll need to be here for some time," Malcolm said as he stood up at last. It sounded more like a prescription than one of his orders. "Maybe a week, or until you can move it without too much pain. Moving the canoes won't be easy. And the hardest part will come first." As he said that, he was looking toward the island and what was visible of the Gooseneck rapids.

Jack nodded. He understood. They would be going back. He wished his arm would heal so he could think for himself.

Jack also imagined that his arm was already beginning to heal. He was willing it to do that. He also knew it would be a few days before he would know if he had any options, or what his next steps might really be.

"Thanks," Jack offered quietly. But, even as he looked up, Malcolm had already set about organizing a better campsite, up on a flat shelf above the gravel bar of the river's shore.

13

By late afternoon, Jack had gotten up to walk. He needed to walk. He walked slowly. Each shuffling step felt like a jarring leap that threatened to sever his broken arm completely.

There was no rush anymore. Jack knew they were stuck in place. As Malcolm had said, they'd be there for at least a few days. He'd set up a campsite where there was still enough breeze to blow the flies away, but where the things they might need were close at hand. The canoes were up at the campsite, as shelters for the two of them, with spruce boughs topped with cedar for bedding.

The sun was about an hour above the western horizon when Malcolm came back to the camp with three fish. They were already gutted and cleaned. A task done at the river's edge so any mess could be tossed into the river and not tempt any animals to come into their camp.

Jack wasn't sure what he should do, or what his dad might expect him to do. This was a new situation for both of them.

Cyril had run away once a few years ago and tried to hide in the bush up from the house. He'd given up and walked home when he got hungry. That homecoming had involved Malcolm's broad leather belt. Cyril had slept on his stomach that night, Jack remembered. But this was different. He was older. Old enough to make real decisions. He'd wondered about the young eagles making their decisions to finally jump out of the nest and try their wings.

Malcolm set the fish aside and got the fire going. Jack took the big tin to get water for tea. He pretended not to notice the throbbing arm inside its birch splint, but moved delicately because of it, nonetheless. When Jack returned and set the tea tin in the coals opposite, the splayed fish were roasting in the radiant heat coming from the base of the fire. A large driftwood tree trunk embedded in the sand and gravel served as a place to sit. Jack assumed things had been located close to the big log for that reason.

Jack was slowly picking his way through one of the broiled goldeye his dad had handed him when he finally spoke. "I didn't run away. I left."

Malcolm nodded, waited, and then said, "People say goodbye when they leave."

"I left a note. And I told Cyril."

Another nod, and the offer of another half of fish. But Jack waved it aside. He'd had enough with one. Good flaky flesh. The bones and skin had gone into the fire.

Jack wanted to say, "You were young when you left," but thought better of it. He wasn't sure where he stood with his father, or how Malcolm might react. Finally he asked, "Why did you come after me? Was it the canoe?"

"I don't know," Malcolm said at last. He avoided further conversation by pouring some tea for them both. He didn't add sweetener this time.

They both drank their tea in silence, spat out the leaves that came with it, and felt the warmth of the fire, while their backs got colder in the sharp night air below the foothills of the Rockies. They had already talked longer, and more, than either of them could remember. Before, at the house, there had been routines and responsibilities that everyone understood and accepted. This was not routine. Jack knew he would have to pick his way carefully through the next few days of his healing.

Before it got completely dark, Jack shuffled his way slowly over to the small canoe, lay down carefully and painfully on the aromatic evergreen boughs, and pulled his small blanket around him. He listened to the rhythm of his heart through the steady throbbing of his left arm and looked toward the fire. He saw the dark hunched outline of his dad. Their conversation had ended. Their thoughts had not.

14

Jack was still in the same position as the night before when the gray of morning and the first few rays of penetrating sunlight woke him. Pain, it seems, can sometimes be a powerful sedative. Pain also sharply reminded him of the events of the last few days, as he tried to move both arms to rub the sleep from his eyes. Suddenly the rest of his surroundings came into focus. He knew why he could already hear the crackling of a fire. He wondered what would happen next. He'd had no experience with just sitting idly, or waiting for a broken limb to heal.

After a short detour into the bush, Jack joined his dad on the driftwood log that had probably been dragged to that spot by a stronger than usual spring run-off.

The two acknowledged each other with a nod as Jack sat down.

Jack knew tea would be their only breakfast. They weren't working. The only formality was that of letting the one who had made it offer it to anyone else. That was the way of the bush and, in due time, Malcolm did just that, pulling the tea away from the fire, dipping the enamel cup into it, and offering it to Jack. What the fire did for them on the outside, the tea would do for the rest.

Jack knew his dad wouldn't ask about his arm, so after a while he said, "Maybe my arm is just bruised after all."

"No. People know when they break something. The bruising and the pain is just a part of it. Your fingers being numb was the proof of it."

During his second cup of tea, Jack asked, "Did you ever break anything?" He was thinking of the weeks at a time that his dad was up on his trap lines in the winter. A lot of things could have happened that would be long over and forgotten by the time he made it back to the house, if he ever thought to talk about it at all.

"There were a lot of broken limbs during the war. A lot of other things as well." And with that, to avoid any more questions, Malcolm took the tea tin down to the river for more water and set it among the coals. He didn't sit down again but glanced around, as if looking for something to do.

Jack sat and watched, as Malcolm sauntered down to the river and up to the backwater near the rapids. There was always fishing. It was practical, and often a necessity in the wilderness. And now, necessary as a way to change the subject of their conversation. Or end it.

Jack was called on to tend a new smoking fire that Malcolm had set up for the curing, drying, and smoking of the fish that he intended to catch. It was a simple arrangement of a leafy lean-to of branches and bush to hold the smoke and reflect the heat of that small fire, so that the cleaned and split fish could hang in front of it. One good arm was all Jack would need to keep the fires going with twigs that he could snap off driftwood, or from the dead lower branches of trees nearby.

By midday, more than a dozen goldeye were draped over a green stick in front of the smoking lean-to. Two of the biggest, and among the last to be caught, were splayed and cooking in the heat beside the campfire. They were starting to sizzle in their own oils and juices, when Malcolm came up with the last of the day's catch and handed them to Jack.

"Hang these and smoke them, too. We'll need them for food when we're ready to travel. We'll keep the fire going overnight."

Jack nodded. "The water's on for tea." He said it sort of like a question, wondering if his dad was ready to eat. His going down to wash the silvery scales off his hands seemed to be an affirmative response.

They ate their fish in silence. Maybe because they were hungry. Maybe because the fish tasted good.

Malcolm finally said, "Two or three days should be long enough to cure the fish we'll need for the trip back."

That was the plan, apparently. Jack knew that his dad didn't expect a response. Two or three days was his plan and his order. He was also suggesting that by then, Jack should be used to the pain in his arm, or at least know how to deal with it, so that he'd be able to help with the canoes.

"Is that splint still tight enough to keep your arm immobile?" It was all Malcolm asked by way of a medical consultation.

Jack nodded. "I can move my fingertips without it hurting."

The late afternoon of summer was getting hot and sultry. Malcolm pulled the tea tin back from the fire. "East wind," he noted. "It will be raining up in the foothills and mountains somewhere."

That was the news and the conversation.

With nothing else to do, they both lay under their canoes and let sleep come if it wanted to.

15

The east wind covered them with a gray, rainy sky the next morning. Malcolm built up the cooking fire not just to keep warm, but also to ward off some of the rain that fell, heavy at times and a steady drizzle for the rest. Jack tended to the fish-curing fire and kept it going, ranging farther and farther for the wood that he could manage with his good hand and arm.

On the third morning, Jack was up first. He felt cold, needed to pee, and his left arm was aching. The sky was already dawning in the east, so he decided to start the fire. It didn't take long to blow the coals back to life, with some of the tinder and kindling from under the canoe where he'd stored it. It was a habit, or trick, that was routine at any time, but especially during days of unpredictable weather. A fire was a necessity in the bush.

Jack's movement and the warmth of the fire brought life back to his left arm, with a pulsing that seemed less painful than the day before. He wanted to peel back the birch-bark splint to see what his forearm looked like, but thought better of it. He knew his dad was the one who would have to re-wrap it.

The first rays of the sun were above the eastern horizon when Jack got up to fetch some water from the river for tea. It was then he noticed the other thing that may have prompted his early rising. The steady sound of the Gooseneck rapids, even though they were a long way off, was missing. And so, too, was the river itself! There was just a muddy, boulder-strewn shore and flat pools of water where the big Athabasca River had been flowing the evening before!

"Dad! The river's gone!" Jack didn't know what else to say or do. It was a mystery to him. Or maybe a trick of nature he hadn't seen before.

Neither had Malcolm. But he had heard of such things in the lore of older folk. And those stories seldom had a happy ending.

"Grab everything you can and put it in the small canoe!" Despite his startled awakening, there was purpose and urgency in Malcolm's voice. He had already righted the small canoe and was looking for things lying around.

"What happened?"

"Something's dammed the river upstream! Get moving! We have to get to higher ground!"

Jack didn't understand. At least, not the river and what was happening. But he did understand his dad. The urgency in his voice and those orders were not things to be questioned. He ran and looked for anything still lying about. He thought of the fish being cured. But his dad had already rolled them up in the small oilskin.

"What about the big canoe?"

"This one's lighter and easier to move! Grab the stern!"

Jack did as he was told. He noticed that his dad had put all their gear up close to the front.

Malcolm ordered, "Come on!" And set the example by grabbing the bow breastplate and lifting it just enough to raise the canoe off the ground. "You lift the stern with your good arm. Let's go!"

There was no time for questions of any kind, nor for further explanation.

There was no trail. This was not a portage. It was simply a matter of taking the shortest route to the highest ground— and doing it as quickly as possible. Malcolm veered one way or another to avoid the biggest trees and the densest brush. But, aside from that, it was a matter of smashing their way forward and upward, away from the river.

Jack, too, put his head down and lifted and pushed through the underbrush. Several times the canoe slipped from his grasp. But his dad forged on, dragging the canoe until Jack could recover and lift his end again. They were both sweating and panting by the time they got to an even steeper incline—probably the embankment of an ancient river channel.

Malcolm said, "Good, this is what we need!" by way of encouragement, as he scrabbled and clawed his way forward and upward on the steeper slope.

Jack wondered if he was helping or hindering at this stage. He winced at times, as the birch-bark sheath around his broken arm banged into a sapling or branch. But he knew better than to yell out. He knew it would not slow his dad, anyway.

Finally, they crested the embankment. It was like coming out of the bush and into the clearing back at their house. Now, because of the steepness and height of the slope, they could see over and through the treetops back down to the river itself. It was maybe two hundred yards away, and down, vertically, maybe fifty. Parts of the river bottom that they were able to see looked like a big, long, muddy ditch with long puddles in its deepest parts. And there was no sound.

Jack was gasping as he leaned into a sturdy poplar. He would have asked questions. He really wanted to. But he also knew this was not the time. He just watched, while his dad tied the painter of the little canoe up high to the trunk of the biggest tree that he could reach. Then he looked up the valley and motioned for Jack to keep quiet.

"We'll try to bring up the other canoe." But Malcolm explained no further as he headed back down the way they had come.

Jack skidded after him, bracing himself and protecting his sore arm as best he could. Going down the slope was even more treacherous than coming up. And more dangerous for his injured limb.

Malcolm listened intently at the base of the hill as they stood beside the big canoe. He was listening for any sound that the river upstream might be moving again. Just how far up it might have been blocked, however, was still a mystery.

All Jack could think of, as he looked out at where the river had been, was the time he and Cyril had let loose an old beaver dam one spring day a few years ago. He remembered how they had cheered when the water surged through the breech they had made. He also remembered being amazed at how much water filled the channel below and how much debris it moved. He began to understand the urgency in his dad's voice. But that was all he had time to do.

"Let's go!" Malcolm shouted, as he heaved at the big canoe and pointed the bow up the slope.

Jack jumped into line at his position at the stern and did his best, as they slithered and lifted the canoe forward. It was a freighter. Well over twenty feet long and broad at the beam to match. Its cedar ribs and planking had soaked up a lot of water.

It was certainly more than twice the weight of the smaller canoe.

Even Malcolm had to stop and catch his breath at the base of the steeper slope. He was doubled over, with his hands resting on his knees, forcing the air in and out of his burning lungs.

Jack wondered if it might not be easier to wait until the river filled again and then simply float the big canoe. He also knew better than to question his dad's experience, or his orders.

Finally, Malcolm was able to straighten again, and made as if to haul the canoe up the steeper slope. But even as he began, he motioned for Jack to keep quiet.

Far off, Jack could hear the sound that brought back an ancient memory, of the roar of the transcontinental trains coming out of the tunnel near Brûlé. Back then, it had been the sound of the world, the sound of the biggest things that moved, the sound of a million tons of freight being dragged along an unending highway of steel.

"Move!" Malcolm yelled, as he heaved on the canoe and began threading and dragging it up the steep slope.

Jack moved and put all his strength against the stern of the big canoe, using his legs like levers to pry against its mass. For an eternity, they pulled and pried and heaved, not even wasting energy to yell out the curses their minds screamed. But on the steeper slope, and in the tangles of underbrush, that eternity only got them a couple of canoe lengths upward.

"Dad!" Jack yelled, as he heard the first waves of the newborn river begin to thunder through the Gooseneck beyond the island.

"Move!" Malcolm yelled. "No! You! Just you!" And he motioned with his hand. "Get up the hill on your own! Run!"

Jack heard and understood. It was time to save themselves. He saw his dad give one final heave as he stumbled past, and then saw him reach for the bowline of the canoe. Jack knew he would tie the bowline to whatever was close and hope for the best.

Pain shot through Jack's arm as he slipped and stumbled. At the same time, he was aware of the crashing, raging flood of the Athabasca, now directly behind and following him. It was a mesmerizing sound that caused him to turn his head and look for its source, despite his better judgment. Yet, look he did. Just like he and Cyril had stared at the rising rushing water beyond the beaver dam they had destroyed.

The only sound that was louder was the sound of his dad once again yelling, "Move!" Except this time, it was tinged with the agony of pain.

And this time Jack did not obey.

Had he not turned to look, he might not have seen the canoe, one end of it already in water, and its bowline tangled. And all of it ensnaring his dad against the tree to which he was trying to tie it.

"Move!" Malcolm yelled again, fearing his son's indecision. "MOVE!"

And, even as he yelled it, the water was rising higher and, at the same time, moving the big canoe they had struggled with minutes before. But now that canoe was twisting and tightening the bowline, a rope that Malcolm had made sure was stout enough to hold a laden canoe in the currents of the Athabasca.

Jack took in all of that as he looked back. All of that and, for the first time, a look of fear that he'd never seen before on his father's face. Those strong arms were now entangled in a rope that was even stronger than he was. A snare cinched by the tightening pressure of the river, forcing itself against the big canoe.

The snapping of a couple of small saplings jerked Jack into an awareness of his dad's pain and peril. He could obey, turn, and scramble up the slope. But, in that same instant, he knew he would be forever left with the memory of that moment etched into his mind. Or he could do something, anything. Jack knew he had no choice.

Jack flung himself toward his dad and into the hissing, gurgling turmoil of the surging water, and reached for the only thing that might save them both. Close to Malcolm's hands, now trapped and pinned to his side, was the knife he always carried with him.

The water was cold, but Jack did not feel it. The current was strong and rising, but he resisted it. His dad was yelling for him to save himself, but Jack knew he had already stopped listening to that voice. He was now obeying his own instincts. And he was using both arms to do it.

Water had engulfed them both when Jack suddenly felt the trap release.

Like mists swirling through the trees with the first winds of early morning, the water of the Athabasca was in the treetops where the canoe had been entangled, and from which it was now carried away like a piece of flotsam, when it, too, was released by Jack cutting through the tether of its bowline.

Both Malcolm and Jack burst to the surface of the water that had already risen above them. They gasped and tried to orient themselves, Malcolm still clinging to the tree to which he had tried to secure the big canoe. Jack, however, had no such anchor and was flailing away and trying to stay afloat and breathe. This was not like the ripples and currents in which he and Cyril had splashed in previous summers, when they were pretending they could swim.

Panicked, Jack flailed about, grasping at what he could. All the while yelling, "Dad!" and, at the same time, gasping for air. "Dad! DAD!" Still yelling, as he finally managed to snag the branches of a relatively secure poplar. "Dad!"

16

Malcolm looked around, trying to clear his head, trying to breathe, trying to regain control of so many things. And through it all, he heard the painful cry of an ancient memory that had never released him—"Mal! Malcolm! Mal!"

But this time he was not in the mud of some far-off Belgian battlefield. This time the noise was not the distant roaring of cannons nor the nearby explosion of shells. This was the surging and tearing of the Athabasca River close to home. The only thing that was the same was the panicked cry for help, as he looked around for its source.

"I'm coming, boy! Hang on!" Even though Malcolm did not know to whom or to what he was responding, he kept hearing the cry, and he kept repeating, "Hang on! I'm coming!"

It must have seemed like a lifetime for both of them. Malcolm let the current bounce him along through the trees until he, too, grabbed the gnarled and twisted branches holding his boy.

"Hold on, boy! I'll not let you go this time!"

They were at the crest of the flooding tide that had swept down the valley from somewhere above. A valley that could only hold so much in normal seasons. Now it filled the reserves of passageways and channels dug ages before. The surge had swept before it all the stuff that was not firmly rooted or held down. Stumps and trees, and anything that could be bounced and floated in its current, were being carried along for hundreds of miles or more, until stopped by some ledge or bar or other obstacle. In places, it resembled the windrows of some great bulldozer.

And through it all, above it all, as the water slowly receded, the morning wind began to blow, and the sunshine of another summer day climbed to its normal noontime height.

As the water receded and the crest continued to surge in its destructive course downstream, Jack and Malcolm found their footing on the slope of the ground beneath them. The poplar that had stopped them revealed itself to be an ancient, stubborn tree that had obviously gained its strength and weather-beaten shape from years of exposure to all the elements. Its profile seemed to hug, rather than grow out of, the slope of the riverbank that had directed the Athabasca's course ages before.

"Jack?" It was a question as well as an expression of surprise. Malcolm's feet had found their footing while one arm clung to the tree branches and the other supported the boy, his son. "Jack?" he asked again. He needed to hear the voice.

Jack coughed and spat. He looked around as if he were waking from a turbulent sleep. Then he grimaced. "My arm."

Jack's left arm above the elbow was wedged into the crook of the tree. Its hand gripped the branch above like a white claw. The birch-bark splint that had steadied and supported his arm was gone. Nothing about that arm looked right or normal.

"Dad, it hurts," Jack said as he looked at it. Only the pain told him it was his own arm he was looking at.

"Lean on me. I'll get you out of here." Malcolm said it as if he'd rehearsed those words before. It was the next part of the plan, ordered from somewhere in the dimness of his struggling mind. A mind that told him to go down into the battlefield trenches for safety, while at the same time, it urged him to go up the slope and into the sunlight for the same reason. Then, still puzzled by it all, he said, "I'm glad I found you this time."

As Jack reached out to steady himself, he noticed that his left arm was obviously still alive. "It's bleeding," he said, noticing the trickle of blood running down from his left hand, feeling its warmth, and then the familiar aching, throbbing from the bruising and the break. And maybe because of that he added, "It really hurts this time."

Jack yelled out in pain, as Malcolm lifted his broken arm out of the crotch of the tree. He tried to be gentle and offer support. And, as he did so, he noticed the green of the poplar leaves rattling in the breeze above them. He also noticed that the boy he was helping was Jack, his son. This was not the urgency of battle, but the urgency of home.

At last, Malcolm said, "We'll be all right. The flooding's over. But we'll have to get up out of this wet and mud. Can you walk?"

Jack nodded. He tested the ground and the slope of it with both feet, nodded again and said, "Yes, I think so."

"We'll go up to where the little canoe is. There's no rush this time." Malcolm led the way slowly, helping.

Jack started to follow but looked around for the big canoe, wondering if it might be stranded in the trees and visible. And, more importantly, still usable. He decided not to mention it or ask about it. He cradled his left arm and cautiously followed his dad up the slope. Blood was trickling down his suspended left arm and dropping off at the elbow.

17

The little canoe was as they had left it at the top of the ridge in a small clearing. It looked strangely out of place, being tied to a tree and all.

Malcolm pulled a blanket out of the canoe to drape over Jack. "Sit here in the sunshine," he suggested. "I'll get a fire started."

Whatever the circumstances or the season, a fire was the central component of a campsite. It represented security. It meant that you were in control.

Jack shivered uncontrollably and his face was pallid. He was propped up against a tree, legs splayed out in front of him, head down. He was looking at his bleeding hand, trying to remember the details of how it had happened, when his dad offered him a small tin of the sweetened condensed milk. A couple of holes in the top let him suck at its contents.

When he'd built the fire, Malcolm came back and said, "Now let's see that broken arm." And as the bleeding became more noticeable, "How did you get that cut? It looks deep."

"I couldn't see underwater. I could only feel the rope wrapped around you and your arms," Jack stuttered through chattering teeth. "It was so cold, I didn't feel anything at the time."

"Well, Jack, you got me free. Thanks."

It was the first time in a long time that Jack had heard his dad use his name. It was probably a lot longer since he'd been thanked for anything.

"I think I dropped your knife," Jack stuttered. "It was the only thing big enough and sharp enough."

Malcolm had noticed and wondered about his big hunting knife. He nodded and said, "But we're both all right. At least for now, anyway."

The cut was between Jack's thumb and forefinger. It was deep, but straight and clean. Malcolm cut a small square from a shirt tail with his pocketknife to keep it covered and closed.

"Hold that on the cut while I get that break looked after. And keep sipping that milk."

It was more medical advice than Malcolm had given in a long time. Jack wondered about that, as he watched his dad stride off into the bush to look for some more birch bark for his broken arm. He carried the ax to do that job.

As he watched, Jack tried to remember about the canoe, the rope, and the power of the rising water. It came back like a dream in flashing bursts of light. The kind of dream from which you wake up in a tangle of blankets and quilts, wondering what happened.

In the same way, Malcolm remembered Jack fighting against that rope, struggling to free his arms and hands, groping for the only thing that would save them both—the keen and reliable steel of his hunting knife. It was like the stories Malcolm had heard long ago. Stories that were multiplied by the war in which he, like so many others, was trapped by the power of history. Stories they could share among themselves, but which they knew others would not understand or believe. The others had not been there.

Jack was sitting cross-legged by the fire when Malcolm returned with the coils of birch bark. He used some strips of blanket like before, and then wound the bark in place to immobilize the arm, and also cover the cut on his hand. As he worked, he noticed that Jack's color seemed to be returning.

"You're almost as good as you were," Malcolm muttered by way of conversation, as he finished tying things securely. "Just a few more bruises on your arm to go along with that break."

The sun, the fire, and their activity had dried them both. Jack felt like he had just wakened. He was stiff and sore, his head muddled with the confusion of trying to remember. He looked toward the slope and the river, now somewhere below. "That was bigger than any spring break-up, wasn't it?" he said.

Malcolm knew what he was asking. "Spring break-ups just involve ice, and sometimes the river getting plugged with it. This was more than ice. Even ice from still high up in the mountains somewhere."

Then, having said that and realizing its implications, he added, "This was something bigger, upstream somewhere. And we may not have been the only ones caught up in it."

Jack understood and remembered the beaver dam of a few summers before. "You mean, this might have done something back at the house?"

"It depends on where the blockage happened. But no. Our house is up as high as we are here. Higher."

"You mean Hinton? Or even Jasper? Or the railway bridges?"

Malcolm shook his head. Then he cut off any further conversation. "Maybe. No! We can't speculate about things like that. We don't know. And worrying won't change things."

Malcolm snarled in anger this time. Snarled at the uncontrollable possibilities, at the memories that were coming back. Snarled because, once again, he had not been able to control very much.

18

It was strangely silent in the little log house in the clearing, on the plateau above the Athabasca River, during the days of waiting and wondering. Both Cyril and Amelia knew that their mom was troubled by waiting. They did not know mothers did that when one of their children was away from them, or when they sensed that their family was being torn apart.

It was Cyril who mentioned one evening that the river below their place seemed to be smaller and narrower. He'd taken over Jack's old lookout on the bluffs. He could see a long sweep of the river in both directions. And he could fly with the eagles that claimed this as their home and hunting area.

In the dark hours toward morning, Rose heard the river. It was like the rising roar of a spring break-up several times over. A roar of water breaking through the trees on either shore, and using all the debris that it had collected upstream as a battering ram to do it.

"Get up!" Rose yelled. "Amelia! Cyril! Get your things on! We've got to get out of here!"

In the vague darkness of early morning, the release and resurgence of the big river was amplified to a sustained and frightening roar. Rose knew they had to be free to run to higher ground if necessary. "Find your shoe-packs!" she yelled as she opened the door.

The noise was louder and more ominous once they were outside.

"It's not another spring break-up, is it?" Cyril yelled. "That's never happened before. Not this late."

"No, but the river's flooding for some reason," Rose answered, while at the same time pulling both Cyril and Amelia toward her.

"Will it come up here, Momma?" Amelia asked. "Will we get wet?"

"No, no." Rose hugged her little girl more tightly. "No, I don't think so. We're up too high. But, just in case, we'll stay out here for the time being. We'll know more when it becomes light enough to see." Rose tried to sound reassuring, even though she wasn't all that sure about what was happening. All she knew was that any sign of panic from her would not help her children through whatever might lie ahead.

There was nothing to see, but the sound of it all was enough for their imaginations to conjure up images of devastation. After all, there was the story of a flood somewhere in their readers. Or was it one that Rose had read from the Bible?

After a while, sensing that the level of the flooding, rampaging river below them was subsiding, Rose drew her children to sit with her on the small bench beside the door. None of them wanted to go inside.

Cyril kept looking to where he knew the sun would come up. He thought that he could already see the gray of dawn lightening the sky. "Can I go down and look as soon as the sun's up?" he asked. Even though he knew all three of them would go to investigate, he wanted to assert himself as the man of the house. He also knew exactly where he would go to survey what the Athabasca had done and was probably continuing to do. What he didn't say, and hardly dared to even think about, was that he knew Jack and his dad were downriver somewhere. And whatever the rivers did in one place would continue downstream. Rivers only moved in one direction.

Rose nodded and said, "Yes." They all needed answers to whatever their minds were imagining.

The sun was up and starting to warm things when Cyril finally persuaded his mom it was time to see what the river had done, and what it might still be doing. His was the mind of boyish adventure. He could not understand that his mom might be more inclined to fear and apprehension.

"Come on, Mom," Cyril urged. "I know a place where we can see things without having to go right down to the river." He wanted to see as much as he could. Their trail would only get them to the river's edge, wherever that might now be.

"Come on!" he repeated. "It's not far."

Even from a distance and through a screen of trees, they could all hear that the river was much higher and stronger than usual for this time of year.

Cyril scrambled ahead for the final fifty yards or so. He could not wait any longer. He knew his mom and Amelia would catch up. He had to be first, for reasons any boy would understand.

And, like any boy, Cyril was disappointed in what he finally saw. The river was not the noisy torrent he had imagined, churning and foaming through a restricting gorge. It didn't look much different from the spring run-offs, or the higher waters that sometimes came after the heavier rains in the Athabasca watershed.

"It was just a lot of extra noise," he said when the other two came up behind him.

Rose, however, pointed to the signs of how that noise had been made and how big the river had been. "There's still a lot of debris floating in the river," she said, pointing. "And look at the far bank. Look at where the trees are bent and broken. The river's never been that high, not even when there were ice dams somewhere during spring break-up."

19

Accidents happen when two or more things go wrong at once, or in rapid succession. With the Athabasca River flood the year Jack left home, it had been several things. Only one of them was marginally human in origin. And one man would pay the price for it.

Paternoster Lakes is a name given to high glacial lakes in the mountains. They reflect the ice-covered peaks that surround them, which are the source of their glacial waters. Each lake, one of a descending chain, marks the spot where the receding glacier paused for a while, depositing a rim, or dam of glacial gravel and silt.

Beaver dams similarly hold back streams in the lower mountain valleys. Beavers build and take care of the dams for their semi-aquatic habitat in the poplar and aspen forest regions.

Beavers were also a lucrative harvest for trappers such as Harley.

The Athabasca River was the collector and channel that drained a large area of lakes, streams, and beaver-dam reservoirs.

But it was also a big hydraulic force in its own right, as it tumbled and raced from its Rocky Mountain origins to the lowlands of the prairies.

In the foothills, a chain reaction multiplied the normal and natural forces of the Athabasca River.

The current of the Athabasca ground to a stop, literally, when after years of erosion, it had nibbled away at a high mountain spur by which it passed—a bend with a significant set of rapids in any season. Finally, the last few supporting boulders were eaten away, and a hill of gravel, dirt, and debris collapsed and slid across the river's course and valley, blocking its flow. The waters simply stopped. Stopped, and began to back up as far as Brûlé Lake, a large natural reservoir.

At almost the same time, snowstorms above the high glaciers, and rainfall below them, trickled and then cascaded into the Paternoster Lakes, filling them.

That big summer storm was also enough to dislodge a big section of ice at the lower edge of a high glacier. That iceberg slid and tumbled into the uppermost Paternoster Lake, and was big enough to create a large tsunami-like wave that washed over one after the other of the chain of Paternoster Lakes. It ultimately sent torrents of extra water sluicing down the streams into the valley below.

That same rain in the foothill valleys filled the beaver ponds to more than their highest levels. However, some of those beaver ponds no longer had beaver to maintain the dams. Their breech and collapse also added to the water already heading down to the Athabasca.

At about that time, the Athabasca water trapped behind the landslide began to find its way through the barrier. It had no difficulty eroding the loose gravel and debris of that barrier, with increasing speed and force. Gravity and timing did the rest, as all the backed-up water piled up in Brûlé Lake, and the added torrents from the mountain valleys combined to charge down a channel that had stopped flowing a day or so before because of a landslide.

The weight of one cubic foot of water is just over sixty pounds.

The average discharge of the Athabasca River, in its normal flow, is 27,650 cubic feet per second.

Boys who play with beaver dams might understand a bit of this.

20

"We'll stay up here for the night," Malcolm told Jack. "Maybe two or more, if necessary. Will you be ready to leave by then?"

Jack nodded. The afternoon sun felt good. It warmed and healed. He'd sipped at the little tin of sweetened milk, draining it. And both he and his dad had chewed on and downed some of the smoked fish they'd salvaged.

"We need water," Malcolm said after a while. "Can you tend to the fire while I go down to the river, wherever it is?"

Jack nodded again and watched as his dad plunged down the long, steep slope. He wondered how much water would be spilled from the blackened tea tin before his dad got back.

The river had been Jack's distraction and entertainment as he grew up. Season after season, it presented itself in different ways, even in winter. Even though it might be frozen at its banks, there was always open water somewhere, sinister and dark, and always moving.

It was the spring break-up that was the most exciting. Sometimes it would be like an explosive rampage of water and ice. At other times, the river ice would just lift slowly and then break apart and drift off downstream. It always depended on what was happening upstream, and in the valleys and smaller rivers that flowed into the main river of the Athabasca watershed. The Whytes only lived and worked beside a small part of it.

"Two days," Jack thought to himself. He moved his left arm a bit, or at least put some pressure against it. He didn't push very hard or move it very far. He thought that two weeks seemed like a more reasonable time for letting his arm and that cut mend a bit.

Then he wondered about the little canoe. And, as he did, he noticed a gash in its canvas down near the keel. Even though it still looked sturdy and capable, it had taken a beating from the river. It would need some time to heal as well. He wondered if his dad had noticed. Then he wondered just how they might mend that gash in these circumstances. This was not like back at the house, where there was tar and canvas to make a patch.

There was no driftwood up where they were. However, Jack found dry limbs on many of the trees, that he managed to break off to keep the fire going. His left arm throbbed with every step he took, and then made him wince in pain with each jerk, as he snapped the dead branches from the trees. He had stockpiled very little firewood by the time he heard his dad come up through the bush with the water. The tin was only half full, as he placed it beside the glowing coals in the upwind side of the fire. The water looked muddy.

"You didn't bring much stuff with you when you left." It was more of a question from the way Malcolm said it.

They were sitting by the fire, waiting for the water to boil.

Jack could figure out what the real question was easily enough. He just didn't know how to respond to it, or how much of his ideas and plans he was prepared to reveal. "I was going to stop in Whitecourt to pick up supplies."

"Or maybe stay there for a while?"

"I wasn't sure. I've never been there," Jack answered. "I've never been anywhere."

Malcolm ignored that last part, and its implications, avoiding where it might lead. "Not many people stop in Whitecourt," he said. "Not now. They just pass through. They always pass through. There used to be fur traders back in the old days, on their way up to Jasper, or back down to Fort Assiniboine, and then on to Edmonton. Or all the way down the river itself, and then down the other ones to take them back east."

Jack watched as his dad prodded the fire and looked at the water trying to boil.

"Then there was the railway," Malcolm continued. "That only made them pass through Whitecourt faster."

"But didn't you live in Whitecourt?" Jack knew some of that part of the family's history. He'd heard of people clearing the land and trying to farm unwilling soil. The trees they'd cut down clearing the land had been their only real crop, as firewood and lumber.

"We lived somewhere near there," Malcolm finally admitted.

"And you left," Jack said hesitantly, knowing what he was saying, and knowing that by saying it, he might also be accusing himself and his own decision to leave. He hoped the water would boil and give them an excuse to do something else.

Making tea only served to flavor the water a bit. Boiling the water had at least served to destroy some of the stuff that didn't belong in it, or in those who drank it. Malcolm pulled the tea from the fire to let it steep, and let the heavier silt and things settle to the bottom so they could decant it.

Jack watched as his dad did things. He noticed that he was slow and deliberate, not as vigorous as he had always seemed before. Or maybe it was because he, himself, had grown so much bigger over the last winter. Then he wondered if maybe his dad was hurting, too. Maybe hurting in ways that weren't visible.

Jack had never tried to think about things from his dad's point of view. He'd always been the father of the family. And, willing or otherwise, the family had always trotted along behind him, often trying to keep up to his striding footsteps. They'd gone where he wanted them to go, and they'd done what he wanted them to do. As far as Jack knew, his had been the only real act of rebellion.

After a while, when most of the muddy tea was gone, Malcolm said, "I think there's a little valley, with possibly a creek in it, just off to the west of us. Anything would be better than drinking this." He threw what was left of the tea behind him for emphasis. "And it will probably be a few days before the river settles down to anything near drinkable."

"Is it still high?" Jack asked.

"Higher than it usually is. It will take a while to push all of that water, wherever it came from, down the channels ahead of it." And with that, he picked up the tea tin and the ax and made for the bush westward. "I'll be back with some better water."

Jack nodded as his dad disappeared into the green shadows. After a while, he got up and sought out what was starting to become a trail down to the river below. His curiosity had overcome the pain in his arm. Jack wanted to see for himself what had happened down there.

He stopped from time to time to listen, and to check on his arm and adjust its sling. By the time he got to the height of where the river had rushed up through the trees, he knew he had reached his own limit. The muddy silt from the river was like slushy snow underfoot. Even by hanging onto the trees with his good arm, it was a treacherous trail. In places below him, Jack could see where his dad had slipped in his effort to get water from the river. He wondered how often he'd gone back down to refill the tea tin. It also explained why he had set off to find a creek.

At the point where he turned to retrace his steps upward, Jack stopped to look around. He still wondered if the big canoe was somewhere, possibly snagged by a tree.

It wasn't. But the rope that had tied it was. Part of it still dangled from the lower branch of a big tree. It almost pointed to where his dad's knife was lying, an odd shape among the flattened and silt-covered grass and leaves.

One after the other, Jack and Malcolm made their way back to the campfire. Both, in their own way, had been successful.

"About a hundred yards or so," Malcolm explained, nodding back to where he'd emerged from the bush. He placed an almost full tea tin beside the fire. It looked a lot more drinkable than the Athabasca water.

"Me, too," Jack said, "but that way." He pointed down the hill. He'd seen that his dad had noticed his hunting knife stuck into a heavy piece of wood near the fire. Jack guessed he was pleased. He'd seldom seen his dad without that knife.

"You must be feeling better," Malcolm said, hiding the beginning of a smile in his beard as he sheathed his big knife.

"I was just curious about the river. You know." Jack shrugged and let it tail off. "I only got that far," he added after a while, pointing to the knife. "It was slippery. I didn't want to fall."

Malcolm nodded in response. He stoked the fire, and then rummaged about in their supplies to make some supper for the two of them.

21

It was almost dusk when Jack and his dad ate. Even after hours of boiling, the dried beans still retained some of their bullet-like quality. One of the smoked fish that Malcolm had cut up into it near the end added some flavor. Hunger probably made the soupy meal taste better than it was. Tea would finish their day.

In the flickering flames of the fire, Jack glanced over at his dad from time to time. Maybe it was the lengthening growth of beard and the increasing grayness of it, or maybe it was the stress of the last few days and, in particular, the experience of being trapped in that cold, raging river. Whatever the reason, Jack thought he was looking at a much smaller man than he had known.

"How old were you when you went away to war?" Jack asked. Although, in the stillness of the darkening evening, it felt and sounded like he had just blurted it out.

Jack had never really asked his dad anything of personal significance before. Talking was not part of the family routine when Malcolm was present. But now they seemed to be equals, because they were both victims of the same circumstance. Now, instead of watching his dad and Harley talk by the campfire, Jack felt he was a part of the society the fire created.

"You were in your twenties, weren't you?"

Malcolm nodded, staring into the fire.

"Did you want to go?"

"It seemed like a good idea for a lot of reasons." Malcolm hesitated, mesmerized, as it were, by the flickering flames. "We answered the call to fight for king and country," he said after a while. "We pretended we were tired of farming and signed up for the cause."

Jack sensed there was more but pretended to be satisfied. His conversations had seldom been with anyone other than his little brother, Cyril. And in those, he had been the one whose opinion mattered, the one in authority. Now it was almost as if he was talking man-to-man with his father.

"How many of you went from Whitecourt?" Jack asked.

"Five. We had to go to Edmonton to sign up. Three of us had never been as far away as Edmonton."

"It's a big city, isn't it?" Jack asked, continuing in the same tone. He wanted to hear more. He really was curious.

"Edmonton's high up above another river. Lots of streets, lots of trains, lots of people," Malcolm acknowledged.

Jack almost looked at his dad, but instead let his gaze veer toward the tea tin. He didn't know where their conversation might lead, but sensed that his dad didn't want to get there too quickly, if at all. He felt strangely satisfied that his dad had said as much as he did.

Finally, Malcolm said, "You sleep under the canoe. I'll stay here by the fire. I've got a big blanket if I need it."

It was halfway between an order and a suggestion. Either way, Jack knew their conversation was over. He also knew that his left arm was beginning to throb, as the coolness of a clear night settled around them. After a detour into the bush, he gingerly eased himself under the overturned canoe and pulled his small gray blanket around him. Not an easy task with only one arm. As he looked back toward the fire, he could see his dad hunched beside it, a dark silhouette that might just as easily have been a boulder.

Malcolm knew what his boy had been asking. Talking about his going to war, but probably wondering why he'd escaped into it. *From the frying pan into the fire*, he mused, smiling wryly to himself as he remembered those days of his life.

He'd been in his twenties. Oldest of the five "English boys" from Whitecourt. Oldest, and probably expected to look after the other four. They'd wanted him to be like their guide and platoon leader. But things hadn't worked out that way. They were in different outfits, because that was the way the army had thought it should be. One of the Whitecourt boys even got into the flying corps. And into being killed. His parents never seemed to forgive Malcolm Whyte for that.

Two of the others were wounded pretty badly. Malcolm had heard about that through the stories and rumors that made their way up through the trenches. And they were probably the lucky ones. But some wounds don't heal. And being given a medal was not much compensation for the one who had lost an eye to shrapnel and subsequent infection. "Lucky to be going home because of that wound," some had said. And some of them would gladly have traded places and paid that price. To them, an injury could be the ticket for going home and getting out of the hell of the trenches.

Lance Corporal Malcolm Whyte. He involuntarily felt for the spot on his arm where that single chevron to denote his rank had been. It had been an arbitrary promotion, maybe because of his age, that he had not asked for. He'd felt old before, but in those muddy months in Belgium, it became real when he saw the fear in the eyes of younger men or boys assigned to him, whenever the shelling started again, and again, and again. Quivering in those trenches was not the glory and heroics any of them had signed up for, or dreamed about, back home in Canada.

Jack didn't know what his dad's dreams were that night. But they did wake him, as he slept fitfully and nursed his arm through that painful night. He heard the incoherent grunts as Corporal Malcolm Whyte shouted something, over and over, to the men who were in his charge, his care, in the muddy trenches, somewhere in Belgium as another battle raged.

22

The snapping of twigs and branches for kindling was the next thing Jack heard. The cold of the morning had awakened Malcolm. And the only way to cure that was to get up and get a fire started.

"Look after the fire while I get some water," was the greeting Jack received as he stumbled toward the welcoming fire. Malcolm headed for the creek he'd found off in the bush somewhere.

Jack added more wood to the fire and then went off to continue his routine of waking up and looking for some more firewood for the day ahead. He was surprised to discover that his left arm didn't hurt as much with every step he took.

"My arm feels like it might be ready to travel, maybe tomorrow," Jack said, as his dad put the water into the edge of the fire for tea.

"It's not your arm but the river that will tell us when we can leave," Malcolm replied. "It'll have to be down to near normal before we'll be able to go back up it. It was still up among the trees yesterday."

Jack realized that the river was not like his beaver dam of a few summers before. With the river, everything was bigger and took longer. "How far up do the river valleys go?" he asked, wondering about the origin of the flooding.

Malcolm shrugged. "A few hundred miles up to the glaciers and the passes, maybe. All of the rain from the last few days probably added to the flow."

They sat in silence for a while. Jack held half of the smoked fish that his dad had given him up to the fire to warm it a bit and maybe make it taste better. Fish and tea seemed to be it for breakfast. Jack wondered if his dad had brought enough beans to maybe cook up during the day. He was thinking of a coming meal, and maybe enough leftovers for the next morning. He wondered about that, and he wondered about what his dad had been dreaming during the night to make him shout. But he said something that was probably a lot safer for the time being.

"There's a gash in the canoe," and he pointed to the canvas near the keel. "Is there anything I can do to help fix it?"

Jack wasn't volunteering so much as he was asking, to find out how such a thing might be done, since they had no tar to make a patch and seal it, like they did back at the house.

Malcolm had obviously noticed as well. He didn't need to

look where Jack was pointing. "Spruce gum and bear grease," was all he said. He didn't elaborate on just how he proposed to get bear grease, and Jack knew better than to ask. His dad was more of a doer than an explainer.

Jack realized he was hungry when the fish he'd warmed actually started to taste good. He was about to throw the scraps of skin and tail into the fire when his dad intercepted them.

"I've got a use for this stuff," he said without any further explanation, as he added it to the scraps he'd put aside from the fish he had eaten.

After they'd finished their tea, Malcolm picked up his ax and the fish scraps and headed into the bush toward the creek. Jack heard the ax off in the distance a little while later. He wondered about it, but figured he'd find out about it soon enough. He was used to his dad not explaining a lot of things.

Jack's mind was really on the Athabasca. He was curious to see what it looked like. He hoped the trail would be dry enough for him to go down without too much difficulty.

23

"Holy!" Jack whistled, while his mind went through a lot more words he might have used. The kind of words his mom frowned upon.

It was his reaction to seeing the river after he'd finally picked his way down to it. He'd seen the crest of a spring break-up, and he'd stood away from its high water back home. But this was more than any of that. Whole trees of every size and variety were scattered along both shores of the river, well above the normal high-water marks. Even the place where they'd first camped was hard to find because of all the erosion and changes to the riverbank.

Jack understood what his dad had meant when he said the river would dictate when they might head back. There was no way they would be able to paddle in that rushing current, and there would be no way to fight their way back up the voyageur channel. Not yet. Even the place where his dad had fished, in a quiet backwater, now seemed to be a part of the mainstream.

But that did prompt a question once he got back to the campfire. "Were you building a platform to fish from?" Jack asked. He imagined there might be some trout in that creek and that his dad needed a platform from which to fish.

"No, but that's not a bad idea. Those fish you cured and smoked won't last for long."

It was about mid afternoon when they heard a big crash from the direction of the creek. In the silence of the bush, anything unusual in the way of noise seemed to be amplified.

"You made a deadfall!" Jack said with a certain degree of admiration for his dad's trapping ability. "That's why you needed those fish scraps. They were the bait!" Then, remembering the comment about needing bear grease, he asked, "Do you think it's a bear? Or a cub?"

"Shhh!" was Malcolm's only response.

And Jack understood.

But there was no other sound. Nothing scurrying or crashing off through the bush. The trap seemed to have done its job completely.

A few more minutes and Malcolm picked up his ax to check on his handiwork. Jack understood why he wasn't invited to come along. He rubbed the splint on his arm as he waited.

"Supper, and then some," Malcolm said, trying not to sound excited, as he held up a big raccoon on his return. "Not as exciting as a black bear, but probably better eating at this time of year." He then continued down to the river to skin and clean the animal.

An hour later, a ten-pound raccoon was dangling beside the fire, and Malcolm was rolling up its pelt to add to next winter's harvest. "Fifty cents for this pelt will make the work worthwhile," he commented as he joined Jack at the fire.

Malcolm placed a small sheet-metal frying pan that was seldom used for cooking anymore under the dangling, roasting raccoon to catch the grease that was beginning to drip from it. "You do the other part," he said, nodding over to the bush. "You should be able to scrape together some dried spruce gum so we can patch up our canoe. We don't need much. But we may as well make up some extra to take along with us, just in case."

Jack found a big old spruce tree, and was gathering some dried gum by prying it off from around a gash, when he realized something. *He called it our canoe*, he thought to himself. *Not my canoe, not THE canoe, but ours.*

Jack wondered about that as he scraped at the spruce gum.

24

When Jack got back with enough spruce gum to half-fill the little frying pan, grease from the raccoon was starting to drip steadily into it. Malcolm had also placed the cooking tin by the fire, with several handfuls of dried beans to boil.

"We're down to voyageur rations for our eating," Malcolm said. "Fish, game, and beans. Although I think they often had salt pork to add to their beans."

"And they would have had rifles for hunting, wouldn't they?" Jack asked.

"Probably." Then, as if he was getting restless, Malcolm added, "I think I'll take a look at the river. You mind the fire."

Jack didn't wonder about that. The river was the big, active, and natural thing that wove its way through their lives. It was the only way in and out of the wilderness where they lived. It was the only existing way for bringing things in and out. But Jack also wondered if his dad saw the river the way he did—if he saw it as a practical solution to something—like he did when he sat at his lookout and watched the eagles. The eagles had urged him into the future. The river had provided the way.

The raccoon grease spluttered when Jack added more dried spruce gum to it. He was careful not to let the fire get too close. *There's a balance to everything,* Jack mused, as he found a clean stick to stir the simmering mess while he waited for his dad to return.

"The day after tomorrow," was Malcolm's verdict about the river and their own possibility for traveling. "There's not much stuff still floating down."

"What made the river do that? It was more than just rain, wasn't it? We've had storms before."

"It must have been dammed somewhere and then let loose." Malcolm sat near the fire and checked on the beans, the raccoon, and the grease. He stirred the beans to break them up so they would cook faster. "Some beaver dams got busted up somewhere and added to it all."

"How do you know?"

"Chewed beaver logs. A lot of them. Old and muddied." Malcolm let the facts roll out slowly. "Either the river flooded up their valleys, or they just broke up and got added to all of this."

"Cyril and I busted up an old beaver dam once," Jack confessed, and chuckled at the memory of it. "There were no more beavers in the pond behind it. Just a lot of water." He looked over to see his dad's reaction.

Malcolm just nodded, thinking, remembering. "Beaver dams messed up some of our meadows at Whitecourt. Breaking them up and getting them to move was quite a job."

"Why didn't you just trap them?"

"Not enough to make it worthwhile. We were supposed to be farmers."

"So, you didn't trap them in the wintertime?" Jack asked. "Like now?"

Malcolm rearranged things around the fire so the spruce gum and grease would simmer more slowly, and the raccoon cook faster. He was getting hungry. He also needed a break from the talking. Jack had never asked him so many questions before. Or maybe he had never wanted to answer any questions. Jack, Cyril, and Amelia had always been more like Rose's children when they were growing up. But growing up had to end sometime. Malcolm looked over at his son and tried to remember how old he was. He realized that no matter what Jack's childhood might be, there wasn't much left of it.

"Lumber," Malcolm said at last, as if that one word answered it all. "We used to cut lumber up in the bush every winter. There was a lot of demand for lumber. The railways needed ties, and there were a lot of houses being built. Probably in Edmonton."

Jack looked over at his dad. They'd been talking. Passing the time. Waiting for a supper of beans and raccoon to cook. But they'd not looked at each other. Not eye to eye. Not really as man to man. Jack wondered if their lives, their worlds, would ever come together. Or if they even needed to. He'd left. And that was to have been the end of it. The young eagles did that. Only the old ones ever came back and stayed by the river, didn't they?

"Why did you come downriver looking for me?" Jack asked after a while. And this time he did look up at his dad. Right through the rising, flickering flames.

It was not a question Malcolm had anticipated. It was not one he was prepared to answer. He couldn't say that Rose had made him do it. The boy knew he was the boss and that he made the decisions about whatever needed to be done. Malcolm remembered the argument when he had left Whitecourt. He'd simply said he was needed elsewhere. That there was a war. There was always an excuse to leave if you wanted to, and very few reasons to stay if you thought your time to leave had come.

Finally, he looked over at the little canoe and stated flatly, "I use that canoe to take supplies up to where I trap." Then, "I was going to go as far as Whitecourt."

Jack wondered if that would have been the limit. If he would have been free if he had gotten beyond Whitecourt. He looked down at the birch-bark splint on his arm. It was starting to feel almost pain free if he didn't move it. Could he, maybe, just have drifted downstream? He rubbed it a bit, and then grudgingly said, "I'm glad you came looking for me."

Although he might have said more, Malcolm just shrugged, waited, and said, "It seemed like the right thing to do."

Jack was feeling a bit uncomfortable. He really wasn't familiar with conversation. Certainly not with his dad. He'd heard his mom and dad talk at times, but that had often been in whispers.

"Did you see anything of the big canoe when you went down to the river?" Jack asked after a while, overcoming the pall of silence by asking about something practical.

"Long gone," Malcolm replied, probably relieved that he could revert to things he didn't need to think about. "It rolled and got swamped by the water. It would have come apart under the pressure."

Jack had no trouble understanding that and agreeing with it. He'd had an experience of his own. "Yeah," he said, "that's how this arm happened." He looked over at the little canoe. "It rolled and swamped, and I tried to hang onto it in the little channel behind the island."

Fighting with the river had been an experience the two of them had shared.

"At least you found my knife," Malcolm said after a while.

Jack looked down and wondered how deep the gash in his hand really was, and just how long it might take to heal. It was not in a place that would scab over easily. Maybe it was a good thing his arm had to be kept immobile for a while.

Finally he said, by way of response and maybe to keep the conversation going, "It was right under the tree with a short piece of bowline still dangling from it."

Malcolm shook his head slowly. "I meant earlier. When you found it to cut that rope."

"Oh."

Malcolm looked off to the west where the foothills were. "I was trapped by the canoe, the rushing water, and that rope." He didn't say any more. He didn't need to. They both knew what he was talking about and maybe trying to say.

"I knew your knife was always in the sheath on your belt," Jack said, glancing over at it through the flames. "And I still had one good arm."

"I think you used both," Malcolm said.

"And you got us up the hill," Jack added, remembering, acknowledging, and wondering what else there was to say. They had both done what was needed. They had reacted.

Jack remembered watching the young eagles learning how to fly. It was not an easy process.

Only the light from the fire was left when Malcolm finally said, "I think that raccoon is probably done."

They ate in silence. Smoke from the fire had salted and flavored the rich red meat of the raccoon. They were both full by the time they'd thrown the bones from the hind quarters into the coals of the fire. Malcolm cut up the rest of the meat and put some in with the beans for the next day. The remainder he folded up in the oil cloth with the smoked fish.

Finally, by the light of some dried twigs Jack added to the fire, Malcolm plastered some of the spruce gum "tar" over the gash in the canoe's canvas, placed a layer of birchbark over that, and repeated the process, placing the next layer at right angles to the first. He seemed to be satisfied when he smoothed down the edges and set what was left of the spruce gum "tar" aside for the future, if necessary.

"That should be set and cured by the time we need to travel," was Malcolm's end to the day, as he placed the small canoe back where Jack could sleep under it again.

25

The next day was clear. The weather had taken on its summer qualities. The warmth of the morning sun rather than the cold of the night seemed to wake both Malcolm and Jack at about the same time.

Jack gently rubbed his hand over the patch on the canoe as soon as he had a chance. "That patch seems to be as good as any of the ones made with real tar," he commented.

"It should be ready for the water tomorrow," Malcolm said. "That is, if the river's ready. We'll check after we've eaten."

The beans were a thick, soupy gruel. Malcolm had added more water during the night to keep them from drying out and maybe burning. At least it had served to soften the beans some more. The small chunks of raccoon meat hardly needed chewing.

"How much beans do you have left in your pack?" Jack asked, thinking about the trip that would probably take them more than a few days to get back upriver.

"Two or three pounds. We can always fish."

"Isn't the river too silty for that right now?"

"That's another reason to check on the river," Malcolm explained. "Or maybe we'll have to try that little creek for trout, if it hasn't warmed up too much already."

There was no rush. It was midmorning by the time the fire was down enough to be put out easily, and Malcolm got up and nodded toward the path that led down to the river.

Jack followed and noticed that his arm had stopped throbbing at every step. He wondered if the cut was starting to heal as well.

They were moving slowly down what was already becoming a well-worn trail, when Malcolm stopped at the place to where they'd managed to drag the big canoe. "We didn't get too far up this steep slope, did we?"

Jack thought his dad was looking over to where he'd been snared by the big canoe's rope. He seemed to be looking for some time at the short end of that rope, still hanging in the tree.

Jack looked around, too. But he was searching for the tree he'd managed to grab as the current threatened to drag him downstream. Or worse. Him and all the other things that weren't rooted deep enough or strong enough to withstand the flood.

"You called me by a different name," Jack said hesitantly as they stood and looked, and remembered. "When you came for me, you called me Billy a couple of times."

Malcolm looked at Jack, then over at the poplar that his son, his boy, had managed to hang onto, and then down at the gray, silty mud that had dried on the ground and everything else, up to as high as the river had surged. The slope of that old river embankment was not the slope of a muddy trench in Belgium. Here the sky was clear. There was no sound of shelling, no rattle of guns. There was no yelling of orders, or the screams of horror and pain. It had only been a memory prompted by the river.

Here and now, there was only the flash of sunshine shimmering down through the rattling of poplar leaves, stirred by the summer breeze. That, and the sound of the river hissing in the channel below. There was only him and his boy, his son, looking over at him, wondering and trying to come to terms with the war of his adolescent life.

"That was a long time ago," Malcolm said, staring off to a place and a time somewhere beyond his son. "The river, and your yelling the other day, maybe reminded me."

Down at the river, Malcolm walked out into the brown swirling water, wanting to test the current. "If it keeps going down," he shouted back at Jack, "we should be all right tomorrow." Then he looked upstream to where he could see the island and the Gooseneck rapids around it. "We'll know we can make it home if we can get up above that island."

They walked back up to the campsite in silence. Jack wondered if maybe he'd asked too many questions. Learning how to talk with someone was not easy. Especially since there had been too many years of silence. Silence, except for the orders, and those few conversations with his mom that were often cut short for some reason.

Malcolm strode ahead of Jack for the final rise to the campsite. By the time Jack caught up, Malcolm had already found what he was looking for in his pack. He held up some fine fishing line and said, "I'm going to try for some trout in that little creek." Then he added, "We need some more firewood."

Jack knew what was expected. It sounded like the old days, and he felt like he was ten again. Hearing that order served to shut him out of the world his dad seemed to occupy, and into which no one had ever really been invited. Although, as he stared into the rekindled fire, he wondered if he might have had a glimpse of his dad's world as they talked that morning. Or, rather, as he had begun to ask some questions. And he wondered if maybe he had been prying, rather than his dad having invited him in.

Malcolm's patience was something he reserved for nature. It was an emotional quality that was essential to his trapping. It was also required for fishing. Or maybe it wasn't so much patience that Malcolm had acquired but, rather, a need to be away and in some safe and quiet spot. In the whispering silence of nature, he could feel secure and even at peace. Here there were no screams. Here there was no chaos or cacophony, no artificial thunder and the unrelenting flashes of piercing light. Here he was not caught between orders from above and the often pleading questions from below. No one to beg him to make it stop, or just make it all go away.

Malcolm had six little trout, all about eight or ten inches long, lined up in parade on the cool grass of the riverbank, before he realized the sun was only about one hour above the horizon of the foothills to the west. It was also the first time he thought about Jack, ordered to wait by the fire.

Malcolm thought back to the day when he'd tended to Jack's arm. His son, broken by the forces of the river. Malcolm remembered seeing the long, slender, almost delicate look of that arm and the fingers extending beyond. So different from his own, and yet connected. A boy, a life, entrusted to his care. And now almost grown. He tried to remember if he had ever felt that way before about being a father. About being someone other than a provider. Maybe when Jack was a baby? Maybe when a new life seemed like a new beginning? A promise of hope?

Malcolm shook off those thoughts, as if they had never entered his consciousness. Cut them off in the same way he had always ignored or avoided them before. His task was in bringing back the fish for an evening meal. Doing something, anything, had always been the easy alternative and logical choice.

He gutted the small fish and left the heads on. They'd be a handle for cooking, and then something to hang onto while eating them.

"You can cook these while I get us some water for tea," Malcolm instructed, and then strode off, back to the creek for water.

By the time Malcolm returned with the water, the trout were cooked. The spines were easily pulled out of the tender, flaky meat which, in turn, could be peeled away from the skin. Three trout apiece became an easy and satisfying meal when followed by some steaming tea.

As darkness settled, the glow of the fire became their light. And maybe, as it flickered in their faces, Jack felt bold enough to ask some real questions. Or maybe it was the realization that if Rose could teach them their book lessons, then maybe Malcolm could teach them about the life he knew. Despite being a reluctant father, he was still the man of the house.

"What do you dream about, Dad?" Jack decided to ask what was on his mind. "I've heard Cyril at times when he dreams. He sort of whimpers and kicks. He says that I do it, too, and we've talked about our dreams sometimes, when we remember them. But what do big people like you dream about? Like the other night when you were almost shouting. Was it about the river and the flood?"

Jack looked down after that. He wondered if he might have asked too much all at once.

Malcolm didn't answer right away. He didn't react at all. At least, not on the outside. But on the inside, he just wanted to shut out all the questions. Possibly because he didn't think he knew the right words for the answers. Probably because he knew that nobody would understand. They hadn't been there.

Jack waited, staring down into the fire. "Was it about being tied up and trapped under water?"

"I guess it was the war," Malcolm said at last. "I remember the war." He said it slowly, thinking each word as he said it. And, in doing so, seeing the thousands of images each word brought to mind. And, because of the intensity of that seething, searing time, each word really could have exploded into a thousand pictures.

"It was the biggest thing that ever happened to us, or to anyone," Malcolm said. "And it was a lot different from what we had been told, or what we had told ourselves it would be." He talked slowly, painfully, solemnly.

"We thought we were going to a glorious adventure," Malcolm

continued, staring vacantly into the fire and seeing it all again. "We thought we were getting away from this." He paused. "We wanted to get away from what you yourself were just trying to get away from—the endless cycles of work, hard work, and having little or nothing to show for it."

"It's not that bad," Jack said. Then he added, "I think I was just curious."

"I guess that's one way to describe it." Malcolm checked the tea tin and poured himself some more. His mouth was dry from all the talking and thinking. Trying to remember the war, or to explain it, was like trying to put an animal back together once it had been taken in a trap. Just bits and pieces scattered, and a pelt that someone would make into something else.

"Was Billy from Whitecourt, too?"

Malcolm sighed. "No, just someone in my platoon." Malcolm remembered the face and the features of the boy. One of the youngest. A replacement sent up to the front a week before. More pimples and fuzz than a beard. Someone who didn't belong. Someone who probably just a few weeks or months before had decided to become part of the big adventure in Europe. Hoping that he'd be in time to fire off a few rounds before it was all over. He'd come because he'd heard the stories fed him by newspapers, and decided he wanted to have stories of his own to tell.

"What happened to Billy?"

"I got to him," Malcolm remembered, seeing the details again. "But I couldn't save him."

"What happened?"

In the same way he couldn't end a dream, Malcolm had to go on. He'd begun and he needed to continue. He needed to let the words flow so he could look at them again, to put the pieces of the puzzle together, so he could look at the whole. And maybe, hopefully, understand.

Jack put some sticks into the fire. A shower of sparks soared up into the darkness, trying to escape the heat below.

"He looked so real and natural as I came up to him," Malcolm recalled. "It was as if he was relieved to see me, thinking it was going to be all right. That I'd heard his shouts and that I'd come to make things right."

"Was he shot?"

Malcolm thought for a long time. Maybe wondering if Jack needed to hear. Maybe wondering if he should let those memories resurface. "It was what we'd learned to call a 'Trouble Maker'—a mortar—that somehow screamed out of the sky and through all the smoke to find our position. It landed close enough to explode one of our Vickers machine gun positions." He was staring into the fire now, remembering the details, remembering the big hollow silence after the shell exploded. Or maybe the silence was just the deafness created by the impact.

"We thought they were all gone. It was like a volcano had erupted under them. Billy must have been far enough away not to be blown completely apart at its impact, not to be buried by all the mud, dirt, and debris that got scattered in all directions."

Malcolm squeezed his eyes shut as those bits and pieces of his puzzle came together again, like in his dreams. He wondered if he was talking to explain things to his son or to himself. He swallowed hard to force his emotions to settle.

"He didn't scream," Malcolm said. "He almost sounded calm. I thought I just had to dig him out and free him from all the dirt pinning him down. I told him to hang on, that he was all right, that I'd get him out of there."

He wondered if Jack would understand. Would he know that it was like him fighting to free himself from the river? Jack had told him that despite his broken arm, he'd felt no pain, that it had all happened so fast. And yet every instant of it had been seared into his mind.

"I think I talked with him," Malcolm continued. "Told him to hold still while I dug him out of there. The dirt was loose and granular, like a big shovel had just dropped it all on top of him." Malcolm was starting to sound like he was cold, and shivering, despite the fire in front of him. "But Billy wasn't talking with me. He was gray, staring up into what was left of the sky."

"He was dead, wasn't he?" Jack asked.

Malcolm nodded. "Shrapnel from the shell and stuff from the trench had torn into him. I kept telling him to hang on, that I'd get him out of there, even though half of him had been torn away and buried even deeper in that mess." Malcolm shook, and he gasped deeply. He'd not wanted to see the reality of his dreams. He'd wanted them to be buried, along with so many other things.

"It was Billy that you were calling to when you came for me in the river the other day." Jack stared wide-eyed through the fire, blurred by tears, choking back his own memory and now the understanding of what his father was saying. "You came to rescue me like you came for Billy in the war."

"No. I came for you." Malcolm said it slowly, deliberately. "I did not want the river to win."

"In the same way that I came for you?"

"You should have left me," Malcolm said.

"What?"

"You should have left me!" Malcolm shouted. "You were free! You were up above the river! You had the canoe!" Then, painfully, "Why did you cut me loose?"

Jack stared in disbelief. Stared at his father, his dad. Then, realizing the enormity of the implication—"That would have made you free, too, wouldn't it?" He didn't need to ask it. He knew the answer.

"I don't know," Malcolm said, looking down. "I saw you, and I think I remembered myself. I remembered wanting to be free, to be away from everything that seemed to hold me down, when I thought that I was done growing up. I think I wanted that for you."

"Like the eagles," Jack said. "My eagles at the riverbank. They get so restless that they finally jump from their nest, hoping that their wings will catch them."

Malcolm understood. And he remembered. But that was the freedom of youth and of long ago. "I think it's different when you get older," he said at last. "When you know what pain is—real pain, whatever the source of it—then freedom is being able to shut that out. Maybe freedom is in escaping from your memories."

"But you didn't make the canoe and the rope trap you, did you?" Jack asked.

"No, but I don't think I minded it. I think I imagined that the river was making us all free."

Neither of them had noticed that the fire had gone down. The fire no longer mattered.

"I saw you," Jack said at last. "I saw you, like you saw Billy. If I'd run up the hill and away, I wouldn't have been free. I'd be carrying a war with me in my mind, every day and every night."

Malcolm emptied what was left of the tea. It was the signal that the evening was over. A full moon had risen to turn the darkness of night and the things around them into silvery shadows, highlights, and darker shadows.

"I'll get us some water for morning," Malcolm said, looking at the illuminating moon.

"And I'll get us some firewood before we turn in," Jack added.

He hadn't volunteered. He hadn't been told. He was just doing what was necessary and what was expected. And it felt good. He wondered if that was what the eagles felt when they first realized their wings were working and holding them up.

26

A full moon on a clear night, and the colder temperatures associated with that, explained why both Jack and Malcolm were shivering and up early. Or maybe it was the anticipation of the day ahead.

"Last one," Malcolm said, holding up a little tin of the Eagle Brand sweetened milk. "We may as well use it in our tea to give us a good send-off."

"You mean to get us ready for the cold and the wet of going up the voyageur channel today," Jack said.

"It'll lighten the load in the canoe."

The canoe looked pretty small and insignificant, marooned up there on the hill above the river. Jack wondered how he'd be able to do anything to help move it with only one good arm.

"We'll take the gear down first and then come back for the canoe," Malcolm suggested. "Going up and down the trail will get us used to it and warm us up."

After they'd put out the fire, Jack picked up what he could and started down to the river. He was anxious to see what might be in store for them. On the steep slope, the poplar saplings were like a crude handrail, or a succession of crutches to steady him.

The Athabasca was back to its normal summer flow. Only the extra tangles of debris and the dusty appearance of the trees that had been covered by the flood indicated the power and size of the events of a few days before. Jack almost felt disappointed that there would be no extraordinary challenge. He had not left boyhood behind entirely.

When they went back for the canoe and one final look around, Malcolm said, "Let's go home."

He didn't see Jack smiling at what he'd said. He'd never called their place on the Athabasca "home" before.

Malcolm hoisted the canoe and shouldered it for the trip back down. He explained that he didn't want to take a chance on the two of them doing it, that it was light enough and that he was used to portaging it. "You rake through the fire with the butt of the ax one more time and bring that."

Jack accepted the task. It was part of the routine, too. It was summer. Things were drying out. And the ax was always carried separately for safety. But, deep down, Jack wondered if maybe it was his dad laying claim to his canoe again.

Jack held the canoe in the river and steadied it while his dad loaded the gear and lashed it in, keeping the weight well to the stern. Jack began to understand why when he was ordered into the stern position.

"You do what you can back there and help with the steering," was all Malcolm said.

Jack nodded and understood. It was like his first run up to Hinton with his dad and the furs. His dad had been stronger and knew how to pick his way through the channels and currents in the tough spots. It was also the voyageur way, as Jack learned from Harley. It used to be the man with the experience, the maître, who was at the front, directing and choosing the way, using draws and sweeps with his paddle to pull the canoe where he wanted it to go.

Jack helped by tucking his paddle under his arm and keeping the little canoe in line with his dad's meandering course, in the easiest possible route back up to the first set of rapids—the Gooseneck—and the voyageur channel around them.

They ferried across the current to the bottom of the island. "We're going to look first, right?" Jack shouted as they shot through some strong eddies. He looked over at the power of the rapids in the main channel of the Gooseneck.

"Yeah. It's as important for choosing your way upstream as it is for coming down," Malcolm acknowledged. He was out of the canoe with the bowline before it ground into the shore.

The island was a mess. Because of its rocky base, it was not only the cause of the rapids around it, but also the immovable obstruction that had snagged a lot of trees and driftwood during the flood. Another good reason for looking and choosing their path up the smaller channel.

"Watch your step," Malcolm warned as they set out.

"Maybe you should tie my laces," Jack suggested. Up to this point, he'd simply stepped into his shoe-packs and it had worked out all right. But on some silt-covered rocks on the island, especially if he had to wade out into the current, loose footgear might be a hazard or get sucked off entirely. They might be old and worn, but they were essential for lining the canoe through some current by a long tow rope from shore, or tracking the canoe by wading it through some current or over a shallow gravel bar.

As they scouted the channel, Jack noticed where he'd been dumped by overhanging trees almost a week earlier. He decided not to mention the spot to his dad. But, in looking at it again, Jack could see where, how, and maybe why he'd made his mistake.

At the upper end of the island, they discovered a new problem. A jumble of trees and other driftwood was piled there, in effect, raising the level of the water and increasing the strength of the current. Not a problem for going down, but now not the kind of current that Malcolm would be able to paddle them up on his own.

"We'll cross when we get to here," Malcolm said, pointing with his paddle. "You'll have to line the canoe from up on that bank while I keep it out in the current."

Jack nodded. The riverbank was relatively clear. The only obstacle was an outcropping of rock that he'd have to climb up and over while pulling on the tow line.

When they finally got to that point with the canoe, the rock seemed to be a lot bigger and steeper. An obvious reason to avoid portaging if possible.

"The canoe's light," Malcolm shouted. "It should bounce up out of that backwater and into the 'V' of the current without too much trouble!" He nodded for Jack to climb up onto the rock. "Just let me swing the canoe out into the current, and then pull me to up above this rock!"

"What if the current's too strong?" Jack shouted back.

"We'll cross that bridge when we get to it! Maybe there's something up there to snub the rope around if you need to!"

Jack understood how it should work. It was a simple matter of angles and balance. That, and enough energy and rope to lift the canoe up and over the sluice of water churning its way downstream. It also required a clear path to do all that, both on land and on the river.

Malcolm swung out into the current. Jack anchored him from his position on the tip of the rock, and played out enough rope to let the canoe veer into the darker, faster water flowing in a "V" against it.

"Pull!"

Jack moved ahead, straining on the full length of rope. He was moving successfully.

Until he got stuck! Or until one foot got stuck in a muddy hole left over from the flood.

"Pull! Move! PULL!"

The canoe was suspended near the crest of the drop.

Malcolm was straining to keep it from swinging into the rock. He was dangling at the end of a rope being pulled by someone with a broken arm and one foot trapped in a muddy hole.

Jack began wrapping the rope around his arm as fast as he could, but it was doing little to move the canoe up the last critical slope. He had two choices.

It really wasn't a choice, however. He just hoped that his feet had gotten toughened up enough like they did in previous barefoot summers. With one motion, he stepped out of his shoe-pack and pulled his still-yelling dad forward, up the "V" of the rapids.

Both Jack and Malcolm were sweating when the canoe finally made it to shore. Malcolm looked down at Jack's bare foot and realized what had happened. He tried not to smile.

He just said, "Thanks. Now, let's go and find that other shoe. We've still got about a hundred miles of tough river to go up."

Finding the shoe-pack wasn't all that difficult. Jack had managed to mark the spot by kicking a piece of driftwood to near its location. Pulling it free was another matter.

"Do you think we'll find that place where the river got plugged?" Jack asked.

"Probably not. At least, I hope not. It might be a difficult obstacle to get past. It probably happened up where there was a really big rainfall in the mountains."

It had taken them the better part of a day just to get up above the island. They were both hoping for some flat water for a while to put in some real distance.

After a few more hours of hard paddling, they got to a broad, shallow part of the river, and crossed over to where they could catch the early morning sun. Malcolm had noticed a darkened area of bush where he assumed a small river or creek might join the flow of the Athabasca. They knew that creeks on the far shore drained the foothill valleys and would be clear and cold. Jack figured his dad had fishing in mind. Fresh trout would make a good supper.

27

There was a creek. The mouth was almost hidden by a jumble of uprooted trees and other things. But enough clear water oozed through it to indicate that there was a cold mountain stream up beyond it. There was also enough of a small flat area where they could camp near the creek.

"How's your arm?" Malcolm asked, nodding at Jack's splinted limb.

"It's okay."

"How about the other one? From the looks of things, you might need it tomorrow for poling. The river's braided and shallow up above here for a ways."

"I think I'll manage." Jack swung his right arm. "I really didn't do much with it today."

"Well, you did pull the canoe and me up and around that rock."

Jack accepted that as an acknowledgment that he had done

all right, that his work was acceptable. He mumbled something about firewood and set off to look for some.

There wasn't much daylight left by the time Malcolm returned with a small string of fish. Jack had the tin of water already boiling, and enough firewood for morning and to last through the night, if his dad should want it.

"I didn't know if I should boil up some beans. They would be ready for tomorrow, if you want."

"No. These fish will do. And we've got that smoked fish for morning," Malcolm reminded him.

The trout were big. Four of them. Their markings seemed to prove that each stream had its own variation. The heads on these were big, too.

After a long day of summer daylight and hard work, the smoky flavor of the fish tasted good. Their hunger encouraged them to eat in silence. But afterward, sipping their tea as darkness settled had the opposite effect. At least for Jack.

"Why did we come out here?" he asked. "I mean, we lived in Brûlé, didn't we?"

Malcolm slowly sipped his tea. "You mean, why did we leave Brûlé?" He blew on his tea and took another sip. "The mine shut down. There was no more good coal for the railway."

"Couldn't you dig somewhere else?"

"The railway needed a certain kind, or quality. They simply

opened a mine that had what they wanted elsewhere."

. "So, we could have moved there, couldn't we?" To Jack, work was work. Where it happened didn't matter.

Malcolm shrugged. "We held on for a while. We thought they might sell the lower-grade coal that was still there. But then there was the Depression, and soon there was nothing to do anywhere."

Jack was going to ask about Whitecourt, and why his dad had never gone back and stayed there. But some instinct or memory warned him to avoid that kind of question. Whitecourt had not been the place that got talked about by his mom or dad. Not quietly, anyway.

Then, thinking back to the night below the rapids, Jack asked, "Were you trying to get away from what you were back then, or from your memories?" He was wondering if his dad had felt like he did at times—confined, trapped, imprisoned—wanting to see what was beyond the familiar. Wanting to start over. He looked into the fire, not sure that he could look at his dad, not directly, anyway. That might seem like he was challenging him.

"Memories? What do you mean?" Malcolm looked over at his son.

Malcolm was trying to imagine what Jack was thinking. Trying to remember his own life and what that had been like when he was Jack's age. What Malcolm remembered was being a boy of about ten, and the next day being a man of twenty. All because his father had died and left him to become the man of the house, because he was the oldest, and it seemed to be expected. What he remembered was missing everything in between ten and twenty. He also remembered being jealous of his cousins, who could just walk away from things, it seemed, whenever they wanted to. For them, it was their fathers who were in charge and responsible.

Malcolm tried to remember who had first mentioned the big war back then. He knew that it hadn't been him. But he'd welcomed the chance to get away, and to have an excuse, a reason or a purpose for doing so. He'd become a man without an adolescence to look back on, and no future to look forward to. The War seemed like a happy invitation to start life again.

Malcolm looked over at his boy, his son, the one who would have become the man of the house if he had drowned in the river, trapped by the rope and the canoe. Would Jack have gone back if that had happened? Would he have dared to confront his mother with news like that? A tragic chain of events that he had started? He'd told Jack to get clear, to climb up and save himself. But would he ever have been able to escape the memory of such a day? Or would it have trapped him in his own memories?

"I guess I was thinking about what you were dreaming about,"

Jack said hesitantly. "You know, maybe about the war, or what made you go to it." He hoped that by saying it like a question, it would give his dad some way of talking about what he might want to say. He wasn't sure he wanted answers to some of the questions he had been thinking about, though. Sometimes the stories he'd imagined while watching the eagles back up on the bluffs seemed to have answers that were safer and, perhaps, more normal. Watching those majestic birds had been more predictable than watching the pattern of the flickering halo around the fire of their campsite.

"I don't know that you'd understand," Malcolm said at last. "You weren't there." He stared at the fire. "Even the people who were there didn't understand." He threw the dregs of his tea into the fire with a sweep of his arm. It erupted into a hissing cloud of steam that made the flames cower beneath it.

"It's late," Malcolm said suddenly. "And we still have a long way to go. The mess in the river isn't making things easy for us."

Jack nodded. He didn't know much about making conversation. But he knew that this one was over. As he crawled under his blanket, he wondered what his dad had really been thinking about or remembering. And maybe what he still had to say.

He wondered if maybe sometimes the peace at the end of a war was harder and more complicated than the war itself.

For the next two days, the Athabasca River became an endless monotony of hard work. The wide, braided channels, now down to their normal summer flow again, offered no simple route to follow. Often it was easier just to get out and track the canoe up alongside the gravel bars or along either shore. Even when the river was deep enough for paddling, it was usually on the outer edge of a long, sweeping bend, where recently uprooted and overhanging trees forced them back to the shallows of the other side.

There wasn't much talk. And what there was made Jack think that maybe his dad didn't like the prospect of going back to their place on the Athabasca any more than he did. It was like both of them were wondering what might be in store for them.

Jack's real and outward concern was about the flood. He was anxious to know where the obstruction had been, what had caused it, and what it might have done in the flood that followed.

"It looks like the slide you mentioned must have taken place a lot farther up, doesn't it?" Jack said, when he thought they must be getting close to the house. He was thinking about Cyril and the rest of the family. There were signs in places that the river had crested well above any normal spring break-up and flood.

Malcolm just nodded. Finally he said, "There's a sharp bend up toward Hinton, with a steep wall of gravel on the outside of that bend. The valley's narrow there."

"Are you worried about our place?" Jack asked.

"The house is high enough," Malcolm said. "And Cyril knows better than to go poking around in the empty riverbed when the river goes down. Your mom knows about rivers."

But that was the end of their break and their conversation. Jack could see that his dad was as concerned as he was, but in a different way.

That afternoon, they worked their way up to a spot Jack recognized. He figured they were probably within a day or so of being back at the house. It was a hunch that was confirmed by his dad, when he said they were on their last boil of beans that evening.

They were on their second cup of tea when Jack asked, "Did you kill anyone in the war?"

"You seldom saw what you were shooting at," Malcolm said evasively.

"But soldiers got shot, didn't they?"

"Yeah, but mortars and cannon fire did most of the damage."

Jack hadn't really wanted to ask that. He didn't want to get back to talking about people like Billy. He just wanted to know if, with people, it was different than killing animals. Especially if you were the one doing the shooting.

"Were you over there for all of the war?"

Malcolm almost laughed. "We thought we'd be too late and miss out. It took more than two months just to get to England."

He looked into the fire. "There were still two years of hard fighting left. A stalemate, they called it. Trenches don't move very fast, if at all."

"Did you hear from others that went with you? The English boys?"

More staring into the fire. "One got into the Air Corps. I think I told you that. We could see those planes from time to time as they flew over. We used to envy them." Then, maybe a memory, maybe a story. "Those pilots used to count the planes they'd shot down. I guess it was easier to see what you'd shot, up there in the sky."

He paused, looked over at Jack, and wondered if he was saying too much. Over there, they'd all seen the same things. Things they wanted to forget. Over there, what they really talked about was home. Of getting back to what they missed. Getting back to the people they knew must be missing them.

"You had to be there to understand," Malcolm repeated. "And if you were there, you didn't talk about it. People had enough to worry about within themselves."

"Was it like drowning?" Jack asked after a while. That was the real question. Something they had both experienced and could maybe understand. Jack sensed that in those explosive moments of his life, he might have learned more than all the book lessons his mother had taught, back in their little log house, or even the more significant realizations that came from watching the eagles soaring above his bluffs on the Athabasca. He wondered if he had learned something deeper, more like a feeling.

"I was just wondering," Jack asked again, trying to explain, "if maybe the War was like me with my arm, getting dragged by the river, and you coming for me. I remember yelling, and I know that you did, too."

Malcolm poked at the fire and sent sparks up into the blackening sky. He sipped at what was left of his tea, swished it in his mouth, and spat out the leaves. "Maybe," Malcolm said at last. He said it slowly. "Maybe that stuff with me and you and the river was like one day of war. And it gets to a point where you give in to it. You just want it all to be gone."

He looked over at his boy. Tears were starting to glisten in his eyes. "Sometimes you just want the pain to be gone. And however that is done is suddenly insignificant. You just want peace."

They both sat in silence for a while. Finally Jack said, "You wanted to be free of your memories, didn't you? Was that why we moved out here?" They were as much statements as they were questions.

Malcolm poured the rest of the tea into their cups and turned over the big tin to let it drain, and for the leaves to fall out onto the ground beside the fire. It was the signal that the evening was about over.

Jack had one final question, even though he knew the answer to it. "You've never told Mom anything about the war, have you?"

Malcolm answered with a question of his own. "Are you going to tell Cyril exactly what happened downriver?" Then he added something that Jack would remember—the real lesson. "Sometimes you have to be a part of something to believe it. But even then, you might not understand it."

They both slept by the fire that night. Each in turn added something to the fire to keep it burning, until the first light of dawn allowed them to get up and begin the day. There was an east wind blowing. It would help to push them upriver, and probably bring rain with it. But the thought of getting wet didn't bother them. It would water the garden. They were going home.

PART 2

1

The rain started in the afternoon, as Jack and his father came within sight of their own little river. It was the one that Malcolm used to get supplies up to his trap lines, and along which they ranged on some of their hunts for meat. The Athabasca River's gravel shore of home was a few miles and two bends up beyond that. That was where Cyril was sitting, waiting. Then he finally waded downstream toward them as far as he could.

"I knew it was you!" he shouted by way of greeting. "I could see you from Jack's lookout! We had a flood!"

Jack and his dad paddled and poled the rest of the way, until they were even with Cyril. The last mile had been no more difficult than any of the rest, but the river felt like it had become as sluggish as heavy oil.

Cyril noticed Jack's left arm. "What happened?"

Cyril had expected Jack to answer but, instead, the answer came from different quarters.

"Your brother went off to become a man," Malcolm said with an unfamiliar tone of familial pride. "He didn't have to go as far as he thought he would."

"It just happened," Jack added. "I flipped over in some rapids. You know." And, maybe to change the subject, he looked up along the shore and asked, "You alone?"

"I've been looking most afternoons from your lookout when I could," Cyril explained. "I didn't run to tell Mom and Amelia because I wanted to be sure it was you."

Malcolm had picked up the canoe and carried it up into the edge of the bush. Cyril noticed the big patch but didn't say anything. He did ask Jack about the big canoe, though. "Did you leave it somewhere to pick up later? You couldn't move both with your arm like that, could you?"

"We'll tell everybody at the same time over supper," Malcolm said. "Let's get up to the house and out of this rain."

"The river flooded one night," Cyril said, as the three of them walked up the trail past the obvious high-water mark. Then he mimicked his father. "We'll tell you later over supper," and kind of laughed at having made a joke.

Despite the tears when Jack and Cyril stepped into the house, it was a happy reunion. Amelia made some comment about finally getting some help with the garden. Rose looked down at Jack's arm, but Cyril brushed aside any questions and said, "He'll explain over supper. They're hungry."

Rose had expected that. She had heard Cyril say "they" and assumed that Malcolm was looking after things in the shed. "So, you didn't get washed downriver in the flood, or whatever it was?" She sounded relieved to say it, and quickly added some more things to what smelled like stew cooking on the stove.

When Malcolm finally came in, he looked at Rose, nodded toward Jack, and asked, "Is he what you wanted me to get?" But even his growing beard and moustache couldn't entirely hide his smile, nor a tone that suggested satisfaction.

Rose looked like she wanted to give them a hug, but she held back. She brushed some things off her apron and said, "We could have used you when the river flooded one night. But from the looks of things, you had your own battles." She nodded toward Jack's arm and quickly added, "Should that be looked at?"

"It's starting to feel better," Jack answered. His shrug indicated he wasn't looking for any sympathy. He figured there wouldn't be much to see. Although he did add, "Maybe the cut on my hand should be looked at."

"What did you do?" Amelia asked, wide-eyed, as Jack started to unravel the birch-bark splint. She was looking at the blood-soaked cloth on his hand.

"Dad's knife was pretty sharp, I guess," Jack said cryptically, although he was as curious as anyone about the cut on his hand. The bandage had not been off for several days.

"Yecchhh!" seemed to be Amelia's diagnosis when Jack's puffy red gash was revealed.

"It should probably have been stitched," Rose said. "But now it looks like it might be infected. And what happened here?" She pointed to the bruise on his arm that had turned yellow.

"I think I broke my arm. At least, I felt something snap," Jack said, without giving any further details about how it had happened. "It hurt a lot at first, but now only if I put any pressure on it."

"Well, you won't be able to use that hand until it heals," Rose said, looking at the open wound again. "We'll just put the whole arm in a sling. Amelia, get me that wild honey we've been saving."

"For supper? Is this a party?"

"You'll see." Rose had already found some clean cloth to tear into bandage strips.

The honey became a disinfectant dressing for the cut, which was then wrapped to keep it sealed, and the whole arm was then held immobile in a sling.

"There," Rose said, standing back and looking at her nursing job. "Now we can all sit down to eat."

Malcolm had already lit the coal oil lamp to take away the

dimness of the place. In the silence after Rose had ladled out generous portions of stew, they could hear the rain beat down heavier on the roof.

2

"Why did you go away, Jack?"

Amelia asked it, but Jack knew that Cyril and his mom were looking at him, too.

When the answer didn't come quickly enough, Amelia jumped to another topic. "There was a flood here one night. It was bigger than spring. And loud!" She waved her arms dramatically for emphasis.

"We were worried about you because you were in the canoes," Cyril added. He glanced at his dad and then looked directly at Jack. "You said you'd tell us at supper."

"Mom was worried," Amelia prompted. Then, more pointedly, "You didn't tell us goodbye."

Jack knew that any story would be better and easier to tell, than to try to explain his real reason for leaving. He found his direction when he noticed Cyril looking at his arm in its new sling. "I dumped the canoe in some rapids," he began. "I tried to hang onto things, but the current was too strong. That's when I broke my arm. But I can't explain how it happened, exactly. It all happened very fast. Even some small rapids can be very strong."

"Is that how the hole got in the canoe?" Cyril asked.

"No. I think that was later. I don't exactly know how that happened, either."

"We were worried about you, both of you, because of the flood," Rose interjected. "We knew that whatever happened here would also affect things downstream. And we didn't know where you were or how far you'd gotten." She looked directly at Jack and said, "We didn't know if you were safe."

It was all she got out before her eyes and her tears said the rest.

These were not the consequences that Jack had considered. He'd let his arm become a distraction. But his arm was not at the center of things. And neither was he. Not really. He'd begun to realize that his actions were a part of something far greater and far more serious. Something that was happening to his family. Something that had been happening and would continue to happen. Families had no beginning or end.

"I'm safe now," Jack said quietly. "We're all safe." He looked over at his dad and wondered if he should say anything more.

"Yes, we're all safe," Malcolm said. "And we're all tired. And none of us is out on that river, wondering what will happen next."

They finished the rest of their meal in silence. It felt like it should have been a happier time, but it wasn't. Like with the rain outside, there seemed to be a cloud hanging over them. There were too many questions that needed to be asked.

Jack thought he was happy to be home again, but he couldn't explain why he felt that way. Maybe thinking of it as home was part of the answer. He'd also found some answers to questions he'd never known how to ask. He looked over at his dad and wondered if he might have found some, too.

"Maybe we can have some of that honey on pancakes for breakfast tomorrow," Amelia suggested. "That is, if Jack doesn't need it all for his cut."

Amelia was the first to drift off to sleep that night, while the rain muffled the sounds of her gentle breathing.

3

As the heat of summer increased, Jack began to wonder if things had changed. There suddenly seemed to be more work to do. Work he could not do because of his arm. The novelty of being a patient under his mom's care turned into days of boredom, especially when the cut on his hand, despite the honey poultices, took a long time to heal. Because of that, Cyril had become the second man on the crosscut saw, felling the winter's firewood, while he himself was demoted to the simple task of dragging the little poplar logs back to the house, where they would be bucked and split later on. He only needed one good arm for that.

Jack considered it a challenge at first to prove himself by doing as much as he could. He liked to think that working with his good arm strengthened the other one as well.

Maybe because of his river experience, he also began to look at his father differently. Malcolm's way of moving through each day now seemed to be more like peace than oppression. His orders were now more like instructions and guidance. And he had begun to look at his family when he said things.

"What happened on the river when you went for Jack?" Rose tentatively asked Malcolm one evening. They were standing out by the garden. She had noticed changes in both of them that she had not anticipated.

The children were playing hide and seek in the shadows at the edge of their clearing. They had never grown tired of that game, nor too old. There was no one to tell them it was only a children's game. The game had grown with them.

"I caught up with him because he broke his arm," Malcolm said. He looked straight ahead, hands in his pockets. He knew what Rose was asking, but he didn't know how to even begin to put things like that into words. He never had.

"Was he hurt badly?"

"He'd gone through some rapids the wrong way and got shaken up," Malcolm said. "He was sitting up on shore when I found him. He'd managed to hang onto most of the gear he'd brought with him." He sighed deeply, shrugged, and said, "I just helped him. Then the flood hit and took the big canoe. We waited and came back together. We had no other choice."

Rose sighed, too, then. She knew there was more. There always had been. And, like always, she knew she would not hear those details. She'd once been told she wouldn't understand.

"Dad?"

Jack appeared beside them. He'd been running, with the other two trailing along behind. Dusk had ended their game.

"Dad? I think my arm's getting better. I bumped into a tree and it hardly hurt." Jack pulled his arm out of its sling and waved it to show them.

The three children stood there, smiling. It was a hot evening. Their hair was matted to their foreheads from running around during their game. They'd interrupted their parents' conversation, but neither of them seemed to mind.

As the five of them walked back to their little log house for their evening tea, Rose mentioned something else. "Jack's turning into a man, isn't he?" The signs of changes they had tried to ignore had become more obvious. Rose wondered if that had been a part of what had happened on the river. Had Jack really gone off to find himself? And, in finding Jack, had Malcolm seen a reflection of his former self?

4

The cut on Jack's hand had almost healed. Rose's use of honey as a natural disinfectant had possibly made it heal a bit faster—that, and keeping it immobilized because of the break. The use of the honey may also have prompted Amelia to persuade her brothers to search for a bees' nest nearby. She'd seen bees around the blossoms in the garden. Jack suggested that a cool evening might be the best, or safest, time to do such a thing.

Malcolm was sitting on the small bench by the back door—a cool place to drink a second cup of tea after supper. Rose came out to sit with him and watch the bee-hunting antics of the children.

"He'll have to go again sometime in the future, won't he?" Rose asked.

"Sooner or later," Malcolm acknowledged.

"We've been here seven years," Rose said. "This will be our eighth winter coming up. Things must have changed out in the world. Things don't stand still, do they?"

Malcolm looked to where the children were laughing in their hunt for bees, toward the moving sounds of their laughter.

Rose looked over at Malcolm. She knew he was the real reason why Jack had left. Jack's laughter had disappeared over the last year of their Athabasca isolation.

"Why did Jack come back up the river with you?" Rose asked.

Malcolm was silent. He leaned back against the logs of the house. "He broke his arm," he said at last. "And there was only one canoe because of the flood."

The laughter was coming closer. The bee hunters were coming back. Amelia was racing ahead to tell the story of her exploits.

"And so ... we decided that we needed each other," Malcolm said to end the conversation.

Amelia had run up to them. "Want to lick?" She held up a sweet, sticky finger to Rose.

Jack and Cyril had slowed down and sauntered up behind Amelia. "Can we smoke them out and get the honey tomorrow?" Cyril was ready for more adventure.

"Maybe in the evening." Rose smiled at them. "If you get your work done."

As the house settled into sleep that evening, Rose watched the shadows of the moon rise higher and higher against the wall, until she knew the moon had slipped down behind the mountains somewhere.

She woke when sunlight sparkled off the chimney of the lamp sitting in the middle of the table. Malcolm was already up and outside somewhere. Probably had been for some time. The children would be waiting to hear that the day had started, when their mother attended to the stove.

Rose looked at the calendar on the wall near the stove as the fire began to crackle. It was sometime late in June, or early July. It had to be. The potatoes in the garden had sprouted the week before. It made Rose wonder about other changes yet to come.

5

A tree prompted Malcolm's decision and the Whyte family's next direction or path. Actually, it was a stand of trees, the kind that would have been a welcome sight to anyone who might be thinking about a new log building. They were spruce, in a shadowy little valley up behind the house, a valley that might at one time have been the channel for a creek or river that had long ago been diverted. Their location had caused the trees to grow straight and clear, as they reached upward for the sunlight.

Spruce was not what Malcolm and the boys had been harvesting. Their firewood was poplar. It burned fast, but it was light. Its other favorable qualities were that it was abundant and, once split, it dried quickly. Five full cords supplied the house with heat and cooking fuel for the year.

"I brought you some water for your break," Jack said, offering the bottle to his dad. He'd just returned from dragging a couple of slender poplar logs down to the house. He assumed that his dad and Cyril would be taking a break, before tackling the next tree with the crosscut saw.

"Those are spruce," Jack said, following his dad's gaze, wondering.

"They're nice and straight, though," Cyril noted. He held out his hand for the bottle.

"Do you think we could drag a spruce log down to the house?" Malcolm asked, not looking at either boy, still gazing up at the trees.

Jack looked at some of the poplar trees nearby. He'd been dragging them with just a rope slung around his good shoulder and a timber hitch around the small end of the poplar. "It's mostly downhill," he said. "But it would depend on how long the logs are." He looked over at Cyril as if he might know something. "What would they be for?"

"We don't have the big canoe anymore," Malcolm said. "And the little canoe can only carry two people and not much more."

"How would we build a canoe?" Cyril asked. "And aren't they made mostly of cedar?"

"Canoes are made of cedar," Malcolm acknowledged, looking over at his boys. "But not boats or scows."

Jack and Cyril looked at each other. In all of their seven years out here on the Athabasca, the routines had not changed. Fur provided whatever income they had; the garden provided food they could grow; and the river and forests provided the rest. The change in seasons determined which activity had priority.

"Don't say anything about this," Malcolm said, looking over at them. "I still have some thinking to do." Then he added, maybe as a warning, "Logs and timber could also be used for a bigger house."

It suggested that he was in charge and that he could change things.

The spruce trees reminded Jack of a conversation his dad had had with Harley. They had talked about the old days, before the railways. Harley had talked about the boats on the western rivers. Steamboats where the water was flat enough and deep enough, but there had also been other boats before that. He said they were flat-bottomed and could be rowed, or towed upstream, and floated downstream on the currents. They could also hold a lot of cargo and get dragged over gravel bars and rocks without getting damaged.

"But all of that changed when the railways came," Harley had muttered. "Those railways, they move things too fast. They change everything."

Around the campfires at the meeting place on the way up to Hinton, Malcolm had grunted and agreed. He'd nodded along with Harley to acknowledge that the railway had driven them into the bush. At least, that was one of the reasons.

Jack knew of other reasons now. And why those were never talked about. His dad had come out here to forget them. And he'd dragged his family along with him, floating them down in a scow from Brûlé.

6

Jack and Cyril knew their break and their talking were over when their dad stood up, scooped up the crosscut saw, and headed back to the poplars.

"What's a scow?" Cyril asked Jack later that evening, when they went down to do some fishing.

"I don't know exactly. We'll find out, I guess. I think it's like the boat we came here in."

"But do you know what Dad's talking about?" Cyril persisted. "Did he mention anything when he got you?"

Jack shook his head, threw out his line, and watched the float and the worm beneath it drift by in the current. "I think he knows that I'm a man now, though."

Cyril was almost fourteen, but still young enough to giggle at certain things. "You mean?" and he pointed to his crotch. "I think it's happening to me, too." He was still giggling, while Jack continued to cast his line in the endless cycles of casting and retrieving, as they fished in the tireless current of the Athabasca.

"No," Jack snarled. "I mean, I think he trusts me. Like a man."

"But you ran away."

Jack thought for a bit. "No, I left. I guess I had to prove something. Pay attention! You've got a bite!"

Cyril's float, a piece of dry wood, was bobbing erratically as it drifted by. It was a big goldeye. He coaxed it into the shallow waters and then scooped it up by the gills. That started them both fishing in earnest for a couple more to make a meal for the family. It also served to end any more questions or speculation.

Jack didn't mind. He knew why Cyril's thinking had recently begun to veer into areas of adolescent curiosity that they were both now floundering through. As with scows, there was a lot of speculation about shape and size.

Later that evening, Jack followed the light of their lamp upward to the ceiling and roof of their log house. He looked up at the boards from their first summer and tried to remember what that boat had looked like. It was long ago. At the time, it had seemed very big, and the boards very heavy.

Fear of the unknown and unknowable had caused Malcolm to think of the future. Watching his boys change as they grew also brought him back to his own adolescence in Whitecourt. He'd cursed his father's death many times. It had left him to be the "man of the house" without having been shown, or told, just how those things were done. What had they expected of him?

Now, had turning fifty suddenly made him mortal? There'd been no celebration of that occasion, but Malcolm could feel changes in his bones, in his waning strength, and in his agility. Age was happening but, like his adolescent boys, there was no one with whom he could compare those changes in life. All he knew was that one day, he would disappear back into wherever he had come from. And if it happened soon, and if it happened here, then his boys, Jack especially, would curse him for it like he had cursed his own father's death.

Amelia coaxed her brothers into helping make a couple of scarecrows for the garden one evening. Some flocking predators had already come to rob the Whytes of their labor and sustenance. And since Amelia had the task of doing many of the garden chores, she was in no mood to let pesky birds get any of the benefit of her work.

Malcolm and Rose were sitting out on the bench, watching all the antics of their children. Malcolm asked Rose, "Do you remember why we came out here?"

"You had no work, the mines were closed, and there was a Depression."

"But you knew this wouldn't be an easy life," Malcolm prompted.

"We all knew that. But being poor in a city wouldn't have been easy, either."

One scarecrow was up. It flapped lazily in what was left of the summer's evening breeze.

"We could have gone back to Whitecourt," Malcolm suggested.

"But we left there to move to Brûlé and steady work in the mine. You said you were tired of farming, remember? You wanted to start a new life, with real work, and a real salary."

Malcolm nodded. More to himself than to Rose. His younger brothers had resented his coming back from the war. They were afraid he'd want to take over again where he'd left off. There had been arguments. No, there had been fights.

"But you wanted to get away, too, didn't you?" Malcolm asked. "Didn't you say that Whitecourt was no way and no place to start a marriage?"

There was a long silence.

"Did we ever love each other?" Rose asked in a whisper.

"We have three children," Malcolm answered. He remembered that they had drifted toward each other as a consequence of who they were and where they lived—leftovers from a pioneer society and a war he had somehow survived, but the poison of which he would always, like so many others, carry with him.

A second scarecrow was erected, with shouts of childish fanfare at the other end of the garden. It seemed to wave longingly at its faraway partner. Amelia ran over to receive her mother's approval. Her brothers sauntered along behind.

The conversation on the bench was over. The routines of life and work often had a way of displacing more important things.

"Those scarecrows look like they'll do an even better job than last year's." Rose smiled at Amelia.

Amelia accepted the compliment, and then looked over at her father. He was sitting quietly with her mother, on the little bench by the door of their little house. He had seen the scarecrows and the work of his children but made no comment. He appeared to be far away.

7

The first spruce Malcolm chose was not one of the biggest. Still, it landed with an impressive and satisfying "whump!" when he and Cyril felled it. Its spiky crown was heavy with ripening cones.

"This is an experiment," Malcolm warned Jack and Cyril. "We need to find out what we can manage."

It was already well into summer. Jack had noticed the days getting shorter and the nights cooler. His hand was finally healed, and his broken arm was usable again. He didn't talk about the pain that still shot through it from time to time when he tried to do too much. For the last few days, he had traded jobs with Cyril, and alternated between cutting and skidding firewood logs. He imagined that the days went faster that way.

They'd felled the spruce into the slope of what they'd begun to call their spruce valley. Even so, it was the biggest job of the summer to wrestle a sixteen-foot log they'd cut from it down to the house. To say that they were ready for supper, when they finally dragged that first log to a stop beside the shed, would have been an understatement.

"That's not firewood, is it?" Amelia stated as much as asked. She'd watched Jack and Cyril lean into the ropes as they came within sight of the house.

"It's an experiment," Cyril said cryptically.

"We're going to see if we can make boards," Jack explained. "We might use them to make shelves."

"For garden stuff," Cyril added, waving an arm toward all the things that were now growing there.

"We'll show you after supper, won't we?" Jack asked, looking over at his dad for confirmation.

Malcolm had just hung the crosscut saw under the eaves of the shed, and tested its teeth with his thumb. "We'll see," he said. "It's an experiment." Then he added, "All we have is the crosscut saw."

Neither Jack nor Cyril heard the last part. They were just eager to try something new. They were going to make something other than firewood. For all those reasons, supper was rushed, and they raced back out to continue the experiment.

Some of the poplar logs were stacked to become a platform, onto which the whole family helped wrestle the first experimental spruce log. Malcolm wedged it to keep it from rolling, and then asked for a volunteer to go on top.

"Just try to cut straight down the middle," Malcolm advised. "And you'll have to cut on the up as well as on the down stroke."

It was some time before Jack and Cyril managed to even make a cut deep enough to hide the width of the saw blade. It didn't take much longer for Jack, who was on top, to claim that his back was sore, or for Cyril to complain that sawdust kept falling into his eyes.

"It doesn't look like you're cutting very straight," was Amelia's contribution to the sawyer's dialogue. "Shelves are supposed to be flat."

At about the time Jack suggested to Cyril that they should trade places, Rose came out to offer them all a tea break. No one declined.

"It's called a crosscut because it cuts across the grain of the wood," Malcolm explained to Jack and Cyril. "The teeth are wrong for cutting along the grain. And it won't let you cut straight."

"You can fix it, though, can't you?" Cyril asked, blowing across his tea to cool it. He was still young enough to believe that his dad could fix anything.

"But then it wouldn't be a crosscut saw anymore. And we still need it for that." Malcolm looked over at the firewood logs. "We still need another cord or more."

And with that, the boys' eagerness seemed to vanish. They

finished their tea and decided to walk down to the river. Amelia knew better than to ask when the shelves would be ready. Malcolm hung the crosscut saw back under the eaves of the shed, ready for the next day. The spruce log still straddled the firewood. They had at least proved they were capable of dragging large logs out of the bush.

Jack and Cyril were skipping stones out onto the river, when their father quietly came up behind them. "The one who can skip a stone the farthest will win," Malcolm offered.

"Win what?" Cyril wondered.

"Well, you'll both win something. One stone each," Malcolm challenged. Then he tried not to laugh as they scoured the gravel for a stone of a shape and size to meet their standards.

They were all surprised when Cyril's stone proved to be the most aerodynamic, or his arm the strongest.

"What did I win?" Cyril asked through a wide grin.

"Well," Malcolm said diplomatically, looking over at Jack, "Jack gets to use my rifle and shoot that deer if it comes back to raid the garden. And you, Cyril, will get to do a lot of work by paddling up to Hinton with me."

"What?! When?" Cyril shouted in surprise and grinned even more.

"How many deer can I shoot?" Jack asked.

"That will depend on how straight you are with the six bullets I give you," Malcolm answered. "As for when, that will depend on the firewood," he continued, looking at the two of them.

"Why?" was Rose's question, when the boys came racing up the hill with their news.

"We only have one canoe. The little one," Jack explained. He knew the loss of the big canoe would preclude any trip up to Hinton with furs and for supplies next spring. He also knew that spruce trees and his dad's musings about a scow might have something to do with it. He felt his left arm. He didn't mind not winning the prize of going on a hard, cold trip up to Hinton. He would have his dad's big rifle.

8

Summer seemed to race along after the rock-skipping contest.

"More than two hundred firewood logs," Amelia announced at supper one evening. She'd been watching and keeping track of the boys' activities with the firewood from her chores in the garden.

"We're just stockpiling them so Dad and Cyril can get away soon," Jack said. He knew he'd be the one to do the bucking and splitting of the firewood while they were gone. He also hoped a deer might be enticed by the garden so he could do some hunting.

"There's plenty to keep us all busy," Malcolm said. "One more day and we'll be on our way," he continued, looking over at Cyril. "You can help me with the canoe this evening and check for leaks."

The next day, Jack and Cyril dragged in ten more of the biggest logs of summer, while several new patches on the canoe cured in the sun. They'd left the biggest firewood logs until the last as a challenge, knowing it would take two on the rope to drag each of them down to the house.

"A week, maybe ten days, depending on Cyril's paddling and what we find along the river," Malcolm informed everyone, as they had their evening meal outside. He and Cyril had taken the canoe down to the river, ready for an early departure.

Jack had spent that time sharpening the buck saw. Rose and Amelia had checked the potatoes for Colorado beetles. They'd seen signs a few days before.

Cyril and Malcolm were gone by the time the other three got up in the morning. They'd left in darkness and in silence, but everyone knew when they left.

By midsummer, the Athabasca River is usually at its lowest rate of flow. The run-off from the high glacial valleys is over and, until the fall rains begin, travel upstream is at its easiest. With less flow, there are more exposed gravel bars to allow for easier lining and tracking where the current is too strong.

"How far will we get today, Dad?" Cyril asked, before they had reached the first bend. He was in the bow of the little canoe, and doing his best to prove that he was capable of the job.

"That will depend on the river as much as on us," was the reply that really didn't answer anything. "Just keep it steady and pull hard when I call for it."

Pulling hard seemed to be a frequent command.

Cyril had always been jealous of his older brother, who

seemed to get all the exciting things to do, while he had to stay back and be the so-called man of the house. Jack had warned Cyril he'd get his turn soon enough, that he wouldn't like it, and that the return trip after meeting up with Harley was the only fun part.

It didn't take Cyril long to appreciate what Jack had meant. Pulling upstream soon became tedious, monotonous, and hard work. And, even in midsummer, the river was icy cold if you had to wade in it for very long, or very often.

Malcolm had never really noticed, or maybe never paid any attention to such details, but his boys were of the wiry sort. Cyril, especially. They were tough enough, but that toughness had usually only been tested in short bursts in their chores around the house. By mid-day, Cyril's lips were blue and his teeth were chattering, despite the summer heat. Malcolm concluded that their tea breaks would have to be a bit longer than he had intended. Cyril seemed glad for their break on an island or large gravel bar. The fire and the sun revived his spirits, and the tea and biscuits did the same for his energy. These moments also gave Malcolm a chance to really look at the river valley after the flood. The islands looked like they had been scoured. Trees had been uprooted in one place, only to be deposited in jumbles farther downstream. But it was the riverbanks, especially on the sharp bends, where there had been lots of erosion. Even Cyril noticed. His appraisal was that the river looked messy.

"It will probably be really interesting if, and when, we get to where it was dammed," Malcolm said, as they set off for their afternoon push.

They paddled in silence. Talking slowed their pace. "We'll have time to talk when it's too dark to paddle," Malcolm had warned, when Cyril eased off to ask one question too many.

Camp for their first night was on a grassy shelf above a riverbend. They'd pulled in early according to Malcolm, in order to ease Cyril into their voyageur routines.

"This is hard work," Cyril admitted, as he began to sip on his tea after a meal of stew. "This canoeing, I mean."

Malcolm nodded. "It'll make a man out of you," he added. And, almost as soon as he'd said it, he wished he hadn't, and tried to think of another topic. He'd noticed his boys. He'd noticed the subtle ways in which Jack had changed over the last year. He knew Jack's running away was probably a part of all that. Confusion about things and not knowing how those things happen, or why, and then not knowing what might happen next, or why, can make you think about running away from it all. What Jack didn't know, and what he was probably learning, was that he couldn't run away from what he was supposed to be.

It made Malcolm think back to when he was a boy, and the

oldest in the family. He remembered being called the man of the house, without knowing what the implications might be. He remembered hating his father for dying and leaving him with responsibilities for which he'd not been prepared. He'd been about Jack's age, he remembered.

"Jack says he's a man," Cyril said. Said it while waiting for his dad to say something. He wasn't sure what. They'd seldom talked about anything serious, just the two of them.

"Well, he's older than you."

"He pees funny sometimes. He showed me. White stuff."

Malcolm stared into the fire. It brought back some of the memories of Whitecourt, of school, and of boyhood friends. It had seemed to be part of growing up, to be good and bad at the same time. And maybe that was why there had been secrets and laughter, and boys being men, and men being boys, and nobody knowing or explaining where one ended and the other began.

"I guess it happens," Malcolm said after a while, offering Cyril some more tea. "Maybe that's something we should talk about some time."

They sat in silence as Cyril's tiredness and the glow of the fire started him dozing. The beans for the next day, sitting in the coals, were bubbling. The canoe was turned over near the fire, so they could sleep with their heads under it and with their feet to the fire. Cyril was soon asleep. It took Malcolm a while longer.

9

On the second day out, there were other signs on the river. Things related to the flood and what it had done.

The first sign was visible from a distance. Big heavy birds circled in places along both shores. But not like Jack's eagles back home. These were black and circled low to the ground. The targets of these birds soon became obvious if not visible. It was the sickly-sweet smell of flesh rotting in the sunlight.

"We must be getting close to where the blockage happened," Malcolm said. "Those animals didn't know what was happening, and didn't have time to get up to higher ground."

"I guess this wouldn't be a good place to camp or get water from the river, would it?" Cyril asked. Then he spotted what must have been the body of a big deer or an elk, caught up in some debris and bloated to twice its normal size. The cold water had slowed its decay. Cyril's response was one of silence. He had never seen so much waste or destruction.

"Those birds can smell things like that from miles away," Malcolm said. "Or maybe they simply followed the wolves and coyotes. They probably got here first."

They paddled in silence for most of the day. Cyril had some natural curiosity, but not enough to want to examine any of the things the birds were feeding on.

Malcolm also noticed things. From time to time, there was a log that had obviously been a part of a house or cabin.

"Dad, is that a hat?" Cyril had been looking up higher among the trees. A circular kind of thing, stuck or impaled on a tree branch, had caught his attention. He missed a stroke as he pointed with his paddle.

There were no birds or anything close by but, under the circumstances, such a distinctly human article seemed to warrant a closer look. Especially when, as they got closer, Malcolm thought he recognized it.

"Harley's hat." He said quietly, almost reverently. "The man I meet up with in the spring to go up to Hinton to trade furs. Jack must have talked about him."

Cyril nodded. "Is he dead somewhere?" Cyril asked quietly. He looked for circling birds.

"That hat could have floated here from anywhere upstream," Malcolm said as he looked around. They'd beached their canoe on an almost sandy shore. It didn't seem likely they'd find anything, but they circled around the tree that had held the hat, just to be sure. Malcolm felt obligated to do that much. He didn't, however, share his darker thoughts with Cyril.

Finally, he placed the hat in their canoe to continue their adventure. "I never saw Harley without that hat," Malcolm said as he pushed off and got in. He looked intently at the western riverbank for the next several miles. He also wondered if the cabin logs might have been part of the mystery.

They stopped for the night at the mouth of a small creek. Cyril didn't ask why. He did wonder if he might try the creek for some fish, though. "Once we're set up, that is," he stated, looking to his dad for directions.

Malcolm didn't say anything. But once the canoe was out, the fire started, and the firewood gathered for the night, he reached into his pack and pulled out the fine line that he used for trout. "There should be some grubs under that big log," he said, pointing.

The rationale for stopping was logical for two reasons. The fishing was good, as Cyril discovered. Malcolm talked about the other reason while the trout were cooking by the fire.

"I used to see it from back here on the river," Malcolm said. "There's a hill by the shore up ahead that isn't there anymore. And it's too late to deal with today."

"What do you mean?" Cyril was wide-eyed.

"There's a sharp bend in the river about a half-mile ahead, with a big ridge of gravel beside it. Fast water, too."

"You think that's where the river got dammed up?" Cyril sounded more than a bit excited at maybe seeing the cause of the unusual flooding that summer.

Malcolm nodded. "It was a hard bend to get by. Only one channel. Deep and swift."

Cyril understood. He nodded, too. He knew that you needed to see what you were doing and where you were going on the Athabasca. You needed to have enough time in daylight to do things. He didn't know whether to be apprehensive or excited. In any case, it seemed to make the fish he'd caught taste that much better.

It also seemed to make the morning come more quickly. Or maybe that was because he was tired enough to sleep soundly, despite the discomfort of the ground beneath him.

They were back on the river before the mists had completely cleared, anxious to see what was ahead.

"Whoa!" Cyril said it. Malcolm silently echoed it.

They had just come into view of the bend that Malcolm had talked about. They were both looking at a raw and scarred landscape that looked like a big treeless river gorge. The few trees that were visible on the slopes of it looked like they had been tossed or trampled into those locations. Many had their roots exposed.

"We'll have to look this over," Malcolm said, and shouted, "Pull! Pull hard!" as he veered them across the river to the far bank, to the lowest and safest side of what had obviously been a landslide, and the cause of the river's obstruction.

There was a gravel bar to land on, and a place to which they could carry their canoe, so that it would be well above the fluctuating water. Beyond that, there was a lot of loose gravel that looked like it had recently been dumped there by a giant shovel.

"Whoa! It looks like a big beaver dam made of gravel," Cyril commented, once they had climbed to the top of the obstruction.

"One with a big hole through it," Malcolm added, pointing to the low spot, where the water had finally breached its barrier and gouged out a new channel.

Cyril continued to look around. Finally he said, "Jack would sure have liked to see this. From the looks of things, the whole valley up there must have been flooded. Is that where Hinton is?"

Malcolm nodded and looked over to the hillside beyond the river. It hadn't looked all that high or formidable as he remembered it, but he could imagine the landslide when the hill finally gave way, sliding down and across the Athabasca. He remembered the hat they now carried with them, and wondered if Harley had been a victim in this battle with nature.

"Dad? We can't go up through there, can we?" Cyril was looking at the wild new channel.

Malcolm shook his head. "Maybe in some future year. But now, we portage."

"Maybe on the way back?"

"Not with a full canoe," was the simple and logical answer. "Not even if the channel was clear and straight. We can't see everything from up here."

It took them until almost noon to portage themselves across the landslide to a safe place to put in, above the gorge that the gravel had created. Malcolm handled the canoe, while Cyril picked the easiest way with their gear. From up above, Malcolm had decided on the point of entry from which they would be able to launch and paddle safely. He marked the spot with a poplar sapling he'd cut down with his ax.

"I can hear the river getting sucked through that gorge," Cyril said as they loaded up. "It doesn't sound like it would be very safe."

"No. It's created a big drop," Malcolm admitted. "It will be interesting to see what it does next spring during break-up."

They finished off the remainder of their cold beans, and then pushed hard for the rest of the day. When they finally stopped, Cyril understood why. Malcolm knew where they were, or rather, where Hinton was. It wasn't long after they had set up their campsite on the western shore of the river that a noise in the distance triggered a memory from Cyril's long-ago childhood.

"That's a train, isn't it?" he asked. The evening stillness and a westerly wind had carried the sound of a wheezing and clattering train down to them.

Malcolm nodded. "Hinton tomorrow. And then back here tomorrow night."

Cyril was up first in the morning. In fact, he'd been up a couple of times during the night. The distant noises from somewhere upriver had challenged his imagination and probably colored his dreams. He tried to remember the pictures that might have gone with those sounds. Going into Hinton was like going back into his memory, while at the same time generating ideas for the future.

"Don't get your hopes up," Malcolm warned. They sipped their tea and ate some beans, while waiting for the daylight that seemed not to be in a hurry that morning.

Finally, the town appeared, as Cyril pulled the canoe forward faster than on any previous day. Hinton appeared as a big scabby wound in the landscape of bush all around it. The Athabasca River passed below it. The manmade arteries of the railway, and what must have been a road to somewhere, passed through it. The latter became visible when billows of dust seemed to push a large truck along it.

It took Malcolm a little while after they landed to get his bearings and point out the school and a church.

"And that's the general store," he said, jabbing a finger toward a big building made with real boards and with big windows. "That's where I can sell my furs in the spring and pick up new supplies."

They'd walked up into the center of things, all very new and intriguing. But Cyril wasn't paying much attention. What he was really interested in was the railway, and maybe seeing a train up close.

Malcolm saw him looking and knew what was on his mind. He pointed a little farther up the hill and said, "I'll be in the general store doing some business. You come looking for me there once a train's passed through."

"Which way will it be going?" Cyril asked.

"It could be either way. They pass about every two hours in either direction on regular days."

"We haven't heard one for a while, have we?" Cyril looked excited.

"No. There should be one soon. The man at the station will know. It's the red building beside the tracks." Malcolm smiled. He'd hardly gotten the last word out before Cyril started running. "Don't forget! The general store!" Malcolm yelled after him.

Cyril found the train station and didn't have long to wait. He jumped back from the platform, as a long freight train passed by on its way to Jasper and the mountain pass beyond. He wondered if he should cover his ears, as the train's wheels screeched their way along the steel rails. He noticed some other boys there, too.

They were looking at him. Cyril decided just to let the noise wash over him, as the train passed and then faded into the distance. He wondered about talking to those boys but decided against it. He wasn't sure just how to go about that sort of thing, anyway.

It would be easy to get distracted in a loud and busy place like Hinton, with its important railway. But his dad had given him orders, and he would know when the train had passed through.

The man in the store recognized Malcolm. He was a regular, if not frequent, customer. He was also not too hard to please.

Unlike in the spring, when he brought in his furs for the agent, there was no haggling this time. Neither was there a long list in Rose's meticulous script. This time the list was in Malcolm's head. He had fifty dollars to spend on it. A ten-gauge rip saw was first on that list, followed by a small keg of nails and coils of oakum. And, if there was still money left, he had a few other things in mind.

By then, Malcolm noticed Cyril looking in through the windows, and nodded for him to come in. As he did so, Malcolm realized just how long and far away Cyril had been from any of this. He watched his son's eyes roam over the shelves and boxes on either side of the store's center aisle, and then look up at all the things that hung on the walls above. Finally, his eyes settled on the glass in front of the counter, behind which were the real treasures of the place.

"We'll set our things by the door and come back after lunch to pick them up," Malcolm told Cyril. He'd arranged things with the storekeeper.

Cyril was still wide-eyed and slack-jawed, as he followed his dad out into the street. His eyes squinted at the brightness of the summer sun. They widened again as they went into a place under a swinging sign that said, "EAT," and continued that way, as they worked their way through a meal of stew, served by a lady in a uniform dress, who wondered what kind of pie they would like to go with their meal.

Cyril could happily have waited for another train, or tried to memorize all the things that seemed to be available in the wealth of the general store, but he knew better than to ask. On that day, with what he had already seen, he knew he would have weeks of stories to share back home. And probably more than a few questions to ask his dad, once they got back to the quiet of where they'd camped the night before. He certainly did not complain about carrying the keg of nails and other things back down to the canoe. It was a small price to pay for such a good day.

"Why did we move out to where we live?" Cyril asked later that evening. They'd had a couple of goldeye they'd caught for their supper; beans were cooking for the next day; and tea was helping to make the evening go by, as they sat in the glow of their fire. Cyril had heard answers to those questions over the years. Things about mines closing and a Depression. But obviously Hinton and the people living there seemed to be doing all right and, according to Cyril's appraisal, living in luxury. There was everything and more in the general store alone.

"It seemed like a logical thing at the time," Malcolm said. "And you know the reasons behind it."

"I know what you told us," Cyril said, "but things change, don't they?"

Malcolm waited for a long time. Maybe because it had been an odd summer. First one boy, and now another, had challenged him. Finally he said, "Yes, things change. But usually not too much. Often the things that really need to change are people." Then he abruptly asked, "How old are you?"

Cyril wondered about what his dad was saying. Or what he was really asking. "I think I'm almost fourteen," he stammered.

"And have you changed very much since we moved out here?"

"I've gotten bigger," Cyril stated, wondering. "Jack's changed, I think. We're not friends like we used to be. He treats me differently." He looked over at his father, the man with the beard that was now grayer than it had ever been. "You're not talking about me, are you," he stated. He also knew he shouldn't ask any more questions. Not about people.

They sat in silence for a while. The moon was rising, its light shimmering on the water of the Athabasca gliding by.

"Did you find out anything about the flood?" Cyril asked at last.

"They say it stopped the train. The water came up so high in Brûlé Lake that it almost reached to the tracks on the train bridge."

They both turned in without any other formality, aside from tending to the fire. Cyril wondered what his dad had really been asking. Or what he was thinking. He'd never talked too much about anything before. Life seemed to get more confusing as you got older.

10

Rose was also thinking. Thinking about the expression, "man of the house." She thought about it because of Jack. What did he know about being a man?

"Do you remember why we moved out here, Mom?" he'd asked. It was a question that everything from this summer brought to mind again. "Do you remember?" Jack asked again, when there was no immediate response.

They were out in the garden, weeding beans. Amelia was at the far end of the garden among the potato plants, looking for those pesky Colorado potato bugs again.

"Do you think the answer might have changed from before?" Rose asked by way of a reply.

"No. But I think that there might be more to it. Reasons that you might not have wanted to talk to us about when we were smaller."

"Why do you say that?" Rose asked. Then, almost teasing,

"Do you think you've changed all that much?" Then she wondered if she should have asked that.

"I'm not a boy anymore," Jack said defensively. "I'm more like Dad than I am like Cyril, I think."

"What makes you say that?" Rose asked, after thinking a bit. Thinking about whether she and her big son might be heading into things she was afraid of, and wasn't quite prepared for.

"Dad and I talked on the river. Maybe because of my broken arm. Maybe because we just had to sit and wait until things settled down after the flood."

Jack hesitated. "I think Dad knew that I was older, more like a man. He sort of talked to me like a man. At least, he talked more and ordered me less." Then, as if he was still sorting things out, "Does that make sense?"

"Yes, I think so. I'm glad you were able to talk. I was wondering what might happen when he found you." Finding the boys before in some of their misadventures had seldom involved talking. Malcolm had just set things straight with his belt. It was quick and sometimes necessary. And yet, it solved or answered very little.

"Do you and Dad talk very much?"

Rose wanted to say, or almost scream, "No! That's why we're out here in this wilderness!"

The question had caught her off guard. And maybe it actually proved that Jack was becoming more of a man. That he was seeing things more like an adult. But instead of answering, Rose brushed the hair back from her forehead and called for Amelia to fetch some water.

"We're done this row," Rose told Jack. "Let's just straighten up for a bit and take a break." She made an exaggerated show of relieving the strain on her back.

"There's lots of bugs," Amelia informed them as she brought the water. "Maybe Jack should help me instead of you."

"No, let's see who's finished first," Rose countered. "Then maybe we'll all help each other."

The two scarecrows flapped away in the afternoon breeze, and watched the three of them get back to their tasks.

"I remember hearing you and Dad talk a long time ago, when we first got here," Jack said, as he started on another row of beans. "I think you always waited until we were asleep. But sometimes I woke up."

Rose said, "Oh?" in a questioning kind of tone, wondering if Jack might say more.

"I guess I woke up sometimes because it was loud. It sounded like Cyril and me arguing, sometimes," Jack added. "I think I heard you crying sometimes, too."

Rose tried to smile. "Just because you become an adult, or get married, doesn't mean you stop ..." Rose wondered what to say next. Finally she said, "Well, older people sometimes need to argue and fight, too. Sometimes we get frustrated."

"Is that why there's war?"

"Maybe. But in a bigger and louder kind of way. And between countries. Like in history. And sometimes for years at a time."

"That's what Dad said. They all thought they were going for a few weeks. But it took years before they got back." Jack looked over at his mom. "Did you and Dad know each other before the war?"

Rose laughed. "I knew about him. But he seemed to be a lot older. I was still a girl, I think." She was happy for the heat of the afternoon sun to camouflage the redness in her cheeks, as she remembered those days.

Finally, at the end of another row, she said, "We got married, thinking it would change things and bring back the way we were before the war."

"But the war had changed you, too, hadn't it?" Jack said.

The afternoon ended without all of the potato bugs being picked off the potato plants and squished into the ground by Amelia's angry foot. Neither had all the rows of beans been weeded. It would all be waiting again the next day, like always. Only the bugs got diminished some more, as Jack and Amelia both waged war on them, while Rose went in to cook supper for the three of them. Rose imagined that her conversation with Jack wasn't finished. He was becoming a man in more ways than one. It was only with Amelia and the potato bugs that he could still be a boy, for a while.

Amelia was asleep in bed, while Jack and his mom sipped on some tea in the glow of the coal oil lamp. The occasional flash of lightning and the rumble of thunder, as a storm curled up into the distant mountains, reminded Jack of his experience with his father during the flood.

"Did Dad tell you how I broke my arm?" he asked.

"Not any more than what you did. Something about the canoe tipping in some rapids. Why?" Rose sensed that Jack was talking about more than just his arm.

"I think his finding me that day reminded him of something in the war. Dad mentioned someone called Billy."

Rose nodded. It was a name she had heard before, during the nightmares, when the demons of war bubbled to the surface. Sometimes all too often. They were dreams that haunted, and soon began to interrupt more than their sleep.

"I think there was a Billy who died in the war," Rose said at last. "I heard the name. But when I asked him about it, your dad said I wouldn't understand."

"I think I reminded him of that Billy," Jack said quietly. "I heard him dreaming one night after he found me."

"And he told you about it?" Rose asked.

"He just said he was glad I didn't die like Billy. I don't think you can die of a broken arm, though, can you?" He laughed nervously and, just for good measure, waved his arm to prove that he really was all right.

"So, what really happened on the river?" Rose asked. "You know, with the flood and all?"

"Well, we both got wet, and the big canoe got washed away." Jack looked pensive, as if he was trying to remember. Then he said, "It's hard to explain. I guess you had to be there."

Rose screamed inwardly. Jack had become like his father! Her boy had told her she wouldn't understand.

After a while, a distant flash and rumble brought Rose back to the reality of where they were. She put down her cup, still half-full of tea, looked over at Jack, and said, "I guess you grew a lot older out on that river, didn't you?"

"Dad said the boys who went to war came home as men."

"If they came home at all," Rose added quietly. She didn't say that those who went away to war usually came home broken and bruised, if they came home at all. "And for some, the wounds never healed," she said, almost in a whisper.

11

Cyril was the first one up the hill and over to the house when he and his dad arrived back from Hinton.

"It's Harley!" he proclaimed. "It's a cat!"

And with that, he handed Harley over to Amelia, and with continued excitement said, "Come on, Jack! We've got a canoe to unload!"

Jack and Cyril raced down the hill a couple of times to bring up the bundles and packs, while their dad carried up the canoe. The boys knew nothing could be opened until the canoe was back in its spot by the shed.

Finally, Amelia was able to ask, "Why is it called Harley?"

And Rose added in a cautionary and motherly tone, "It's pregnant."

Malcolm calmly nodded and said, "We knew that. But we couldn't leave it."

"It was almost in the same place where we found Mr. Harley's hat on the way up to Hinton," Cyril chimed in. "But we found her on the way back. Dad says it's a house cat. We couldn't leave it in the bush. We didn't want it to die," Cyril added.

In all of this, Harley, a big orangey tabby, seemed to have claimed Amelia's lap as the safest spot in which to curl up, and was coaxed to produce a gentle purr, much to Amelia's delight.

All she asked was, "What does pregnant mean?"

"I think we'll find out soon enough," Rose predicted, feeling the cat's tummy. Then she added one word, "Kittens."

"I'm going to have a family of them? When?" Amelia asked, wide-eyed.

"We'll know when it starts to nest," Rose said.

Jack was more interested in the other things. "Is that the new saw?" he asked, looking at the flat thing wrapped in burlap.

"We'll maybe try it after supper," Malcolm suggested. "Bring my packs, tools and things over to the shed."

That was the signal for Jack and Cyril to do just that. But, since it would be a while before supper, Jack's eagerness got the better of him.

"The spruce log's still propped up and waiting," he suggested.

"The man on the bottom pulls down and cuts. The one on top draws the saw back up and guides it," were Malcolm's only instructions. "Look at the teeth. It can only cut in one direction."

The saw was stiff, straight, and sharp. The boys continued

from their earlier feeble effort with the crosscut, and had almost sliced a quarter of the spruce log down the middle, by the time Amelia came out to check on the shelves and call them all in to supper.

Over supper, Jack and Cyril laughed and talked about their accomplishment with the new saw, and speculated that they could do things better if they could place the logs on a cutting platform. Jack mentioned that his arm was obviously healed because it hardly hurt at all. Cyril countered by offering him the job on the bottom, so that Jack would be the one to get covered with sawdust. Malcolm reminded them both that this was just a practice log and there would be more to follow. Amelia suggested that once they had cut the boards for the shelves, they could then cut some boards for a bigger bed for her. Then she wondered why Jack and Cyril were laughing.

Malcolm ended the meal by getting up and going out. That, in itself, was not unusual. What was unusual was that he returned from the shed and held out a bag of hard candy for Rose to distribute.

"Whoa!" Cyril exclaimed. "I saw those in the general store!"

Rose let each of them have one, and suggested that the rest would be for special occasions.

For the rest of the evening, Cyril was the storyteller. He sounded like one of the explorers from their school textbooks from which their mom had taught them. Stories about things that always seemed impossible and far away.

Harley quietly explored on her own, and prowled about in the shadows of the little log house, away from the glow of the lamp. Rose knew that soon there would be another real-life story.

It didn't take long. Or maybe Harley had been waiting to settle into some place that looked and felt like her former home, and with people to help her look after things. She even waited until Malcolm and the boys were clear of the house the next morning, and working in the bush, for her to announce that her time had come.

"Mom! I think Harley's sick!" Amelia had come back into the house for something, and heard Harley's unnatural meowing somewhere in the darkened corners of the house.

Rose came in and quietly took control. She realized that none of the school lessons she had taught the year before would be as interesting, or memorable, or practical, as Harley's big event.

Harley was a big mature cat, who looked like she might have had some experience in these things. But practice does not always lead to subsequent successful outcomes. She squirmed and howled and looked up pitifully for any moral support.

Harley struggled and heaved four times. And each time, Rose and Amelia felt the pain with her. Amelia had many questions about the blood and other yucky stuff. Even more questions as Harley's rough tongue began cleaning each of the mewling kittens in turn. When it seemed obvious that Harley was done, and Rose had inspected her tummy to check, a clean cloth was put in place for the new family's bedding. Harley continued to clean her brood, and both Rose and Amelia sighed and smiled.

"Now what are they doing?"

"They're nursing—eating," Rose explained. "They're doing what all babies do." It seemed logical to take advantage of the opportunity and continue with the practical lessons of motherhood.

Harley purred with relief.

By the time Malcolm and the boys arrived at noon, dragging a big spruce log, Amelia acted like the town crier and announced Harley's accomplishment. Then she shushed the boys and ushered them over to Harley's corner.

The invitation was hardly necessary. Harley's delivery was probably the biggest and liveliest event in the Whyte household in years.

"They look like baby mice," Jack whispered. He'd found one or two of those mouse nests over the years. "Except they're obviously bigger. And they've got some fur."

"Mom says their eyes will open in a week or so," Amelia informed her brothers, sharing the biology lessons she had learned. Then she giggled, "They came out of Harley's bum."

That kind of ended the conversation, while the boys continued to look in at the four furry, squirming sausages pawing to get at Harley's teats.

But Cyril had obviously been thinking. "How'd they get in there?"

It was at that point that Malcolm remembered he needed to sharpen a saw, and headed out to the shed. Pregnant cats might provide the impetus for anatomy lessons, but they don't necessarily make them any easier.

Lunch was quiet. Amelia had suggested that the babies needed rest and quiet.

Jack finally started things with another question. "How come one of the kittens is orange, like Harley, but the other three are kind of gray?"

"It happens sometimes," Malcolm said. Maybe he was wondering exactly how much had been said while he'd been out sharpening the saw. "Those three also have short tails. Maybe she mated with a bobcat, although this is a bit out of their normal territory." Then he looked at Rose quizzically, hoping that mating might have been one of her anatomy lessons.

It had and it hadn't. About some of those technical details, Rose had rather formally told the boys, "You'd better ask your father about that."

After lunch, it was a long walk back to where the men

were cutting spruce trees in the bush. Although he tried, even Malcolm's striding gait could not separate him from the boys and some of their questions. His answers were brief and evasive. They had a job to do, cutting logs for a scow, he told them.

12

A scow had brought the Whyte family down the Athabasca River seven years ago. And, as they had drifted, rowed, and steered through the currents to the remote place Malcolm had selected, they had drifted away from other people into a world of silence.

That silence was something Jack had seen and felt as he grew. But he had not understood it. Maybe the silence was what he had run away from while, in his mind, he was following those fledgling eagles he had watched from his river lookout.

Rose had seen some of that in Jack, too. But now some of the silence seemed to have ended, because of what had happened between Jack and his father on the river. Something from which she was cut off because she had not been there, and therefore would not understand.

There was, however, a growing pile of spruce logs in the yard. They could not be ignored or hidden away.

"Those are more than just an experiment, or for a few

shelves, aren't they?" Rose asked Malcolm, after another day of him and the boys dragging in bigger and bigger logs.

They were sitting on the bench, having a second cup of tea that evening. Amelia was busy with Harley and the kittens; Jack and Cyril were busy with a framework on which to cut lumber with their new saw.

"We don't have a big canoe anymore." Malcolm knew it sounded lame and hollow, even as he said it. He also knew there was nowhere to run or get away from whatever might come next. He wasn't even sure he wanted to anymore. Or that he needed to.

"I overheard the boys talking about a scow," Rose said. "I think it's a good idea."

They sat in silence for a while. Malcolm pretended he needed to finish his tea. Finally he said, "Maybe you and I should go down to see how we might launch it in the spring."

A quiet walk down to the Athabasca took Rose by surprise. It reminded her of a walk the two of them had taken many summers before, into a ripening hayfield on a farm near Whitecourt.

Jack had lit the coal oil lamp by the time Rose and Malcolm returned to the house. Amelia and Cyril were playing with the kittens. Jack was surprised to see his mom smile at him.

"Building a scow seems like a good idea," she said. "It was a scow that brought us here, remember?" And she pointed up to the roof of the house.

Jack didn't know what his mom and dad had talked about, but she seemed to be giving him the credit for it. It made him feel older, more adult.

13

It seemed like summer was disappearing while they weren't looking. The garden had exploded with beans and a lot of other things. There were more than enough fresh things to eat.

Jack and Cyril had stockpiled enough spruce logs to let them set to work, producing the boards that began to look more and more like a real stack of lumber. They imagined that on good days, they might be able to produce one sixteen-foot board per day. They didn't say whether that included squaring up the logs or not.

All of which gave Malcolm time to use the canoe to bring most of his supplies up to his trapping cabin for the coming winter.

There were still six large logs in the bush by the time of the first snow. "It's all part of the plan, Mom," Jack assured Rose, with the kind of swagger that seemed to come with size and his increasing sense of self-worth.

Jack could not help but notice that things had changed

in the routines of the Whytes' hermitage household in the Athabasca woods. There now seemed to be a purpose to their lives. Before, they had gone from season to season, with each annual cycle being a repetition of the one before. But now, the next spring, or early summer at the latest, would see them haul and slide a scow down to the river. It would be a time of travel, or even departure, he imagined. His dad had mentioned a fur auction in Edmonton. They were like emigrants anticipating a new country and a new culture.

For Jack, Cyril, and Amelia, it would be almost as dramatic as that. Even Jack had already spent more than half his lifetime where they were. But, in the next year, like Harley with her kittens, they would be born into a world that would be new and strange.

Edmonton seemed to be their target, or goal—big enough to absorb a new family without them being noticed. Malcolm had said that a good harvest of furs in the coming winter would be needed. They had no other finances.

"I'll be back in two weeks or so," Malcolm said on the first day of his trapping activities. There was enough snow on the ground to cause him to use snowshoes on the trail up to the trap lines, more than ten miles back into the bush and up into the first foothill valley. It was the first time his going up there seemed to warrant more than just packing up and shutting the door behind him.

"You be careful up there," was Rose's goodbye.

"When can I come up to help?" Jack wondered.

"You're needed here. You and Cyril have a pile of spruce to work on."

The trap lines were Malcolm's work and his sanctuary. Another level, another step farther away from everything that he had tried to leave seven years before.

And now Jack wondered if that was what it had been like for Mr. Harley—if the wilderness had been that man's escape from things he could not understand but which, from time to time, seemed to overwhelm him.

Jack stood and watched longer than the rest. Watched long after his dad had disappeared into the forested darkness of winter, on the trail up to his trap lines.

14

"We're going hunting!"

Jack and Cyril had practically crashed through the door, with Jack making the announcement and Cyril nodding in eager support.

"It's good fall meat," Cyril added, shaking the sawdust off himself.

Jack and Cyril had been busy for most of the morning with their spruce logs and lumber. However, as interesting as sawing might have been at first, after a steady week of it, it had become real work. Hard work, as they often repeated at almost every meal. But, on this workday, a deer walking by at the far end of the garden was an invitation to do something else.

"I saw it from up on the saw pit," Jack explained. "A big buck that looked like it was going to follow our trail up to the spruce woods."

"But your dad has the rifle, doesn't he?" Rose asked.

"He just took the .22 this time," Cyril said. "He had too many traps to carry and didn't want the extra weight of the big rifle. Right, Jack?"

Jack nodded, and used his best argument to seal the deal, so to speak. "I still have six shells that I didn't use when Dad and Cyril went up to Hinton, remember? I was supposed to use them to keep deer from your garden, Mom."

"Yeah, they were for deer," Cyril said eagerly. "And this is definitely a deer."

"And we do need meat. And it's cold enough to keep it now." Jack said, as if there could be no argument. He could have said more, if needed.

He was taller than his mom. Had been for some time. And he was the man of the house. But, more than that, since the events on the river early in the summer, he'd become like his dad's second in command.

More than a foot of snow muffled any noise they might make tracking the big buck. Once they got to the edge of the clearing, Jack had little difficulty picking up the deer's prints.

"If you want to lead, you'll have to carry the gun," Jack warned Cyril in a hoarse whisper. "That's the rule, remember? You don't want to get shot in the back if I trip or stumble, do you?"

Cyril obeyed his brother and the logic of trailing behind, all the while looking impatiently in all directions.

Jack used both arms to carry the big .303 Ross rifle. His dad hadn't said much about it, except that it was an army surplus rifle that was cheap and affordable, even in a Depression.

"It shoots straight, far, and hard," Malcolm had told Jack once during a hunt. He didn't add that in the muddy trenches of the World War, it had a reputation for jamming. It had been replaced by a more standard military rifle. "Keep it clean," Malcolm said as a warning, and showed Jack how.

All of which explained why Jack often did just that, whether the rifle had been used or not. Like sharpening the new saw, it was something in which he took pride.

"We really do need meat, don't we?" Cyril whispered as they trudged along.

"Yeah. Dad hasn't had time to go hunting yet. And the weather's been too warm," Jack whispered. "Now, shut up. He can't be far. He's walking slowly from the looks of his tracks."

It was a clear day, with a slight breeze coming toward them. They would be out of the poplars soon and into the grove of spruce and other conifers of their so-called lumbering valley. Jack motioned for them to stop every hundred yards or so. By standing still, they would be better able to see anything else that moved.

"Look for something horizontal," Jack whispered. "Something at right angles to the tree trunks. That'll be the back of the deer. It stands out because it's flat."

The big buck had stopped to browse on some dry grass he'd kicked loose, under the snow on a rise. Both boys saw it and, aside from Jack slowly settling to one knee and raising the rifle, they were motionless. A head shot would have been a clean kill. But the deer was feeding, and its head moved unpredictably. Jack took the sure shot, like his dad had taught him, and fired. One shot, even from three hundred feet, was all it took. The deer crumpled where it stood.

"Wow! That was loud!" Cyril exclaimed. "And it was good. One shot! You got him!"

"Let's make sure," Jack said, trembling as he rose. "I guess we can make some noise now," he grinned.

After they raced up to the deer, they noticed it had been a crippling shot, up in the shoulders. The deer was still struggling.

"I can finish it," Cyril pleaded. "You said I could have a shot. Dad let you shoot that rifle when you were thirteen."

Jack looked back and forth between the buck he'd hunted and shot and his little brother. He was in a position to make decisions. He could be generous and let Cyril take some of the credit.

"All right," Jack said at last, feigning reluctance. "You know where to aim, right?"

Cyril nodded and accepted the rifle. It suddenly looked bigger and felt heavier than he remembered, from when he'd watched and helped Jack clean it. Just to be ready.

"I didn't eject the shell," Jack reminded him. Another safety lesson—let the one firing the gun be the one to load it. "There's another two rounds in the magazine."

Cyril had thrown his mitts to the ground and nervously pulled back, and then pushed forward, on the bolt of the rifle. He took a deep breath, relaxed, aimed, and fired.

Jack was looking at the deer and saw that the shot had reached its mark as expected. What he had not expected after the sound of the gun firing, was the long second of silence, and then a scream of unmistakable terror from Cyril.

The rifle landed with a "whump" in the snow, its gaping chamber still emitting a trail of smoke from the shot. It fell because Cyril instinctively reached up to cover the throbbing, bleeding wound on his face, before he fell to his knees and then settled into the snow.

"What happened? What did you do?!" It was a question of fear rather than one of objective enquiry.

Cyril didn't answer. He howled in pain and at the horror of tasting the rustiness of his blood. He couldn't see any of this, because his eyes were still squeezed tightly shut.

"What happened?" Jack asked again, more quietly now, but no less urgently. Then he saw the bolt of the rifle, back from the breech, where it didn't belong. He realized then that he hadn't heard the rifle fire, but explode.

Jack knelt beside his brother to support him and to see what there was to see.

"Aᴀᴀᴀaaahhh! It hurts!" Cyril continued to wail.

Jack could understand that. He saw the blood. He could remember searing pain. "I can't see," Jack told Cyril. "Lift your hand and let me see how bad it is."

"It's bad! It feels bad! And it hurts!" Cyril finally screamed. Then he repeated Jack's question, "What happened?"

"The rifle misfired or exploded or something." Jack was going to ask again about what Cyril had done to cause that but decided against it. Cyril's wound was the immediate problem that needed to be solved. They had to get home.

"Here," Jack said, "hold the back of your mitt over it. It's soft and pretty clean." Then, more slowly, he asked, "Can you walk?"

"I think so," Cyril burbled through his blood. Jack had already begun to lift and steady him.

There was no alternative. They had to get back to the house. The gun shots would have been heard there, but a hunt only ends when the animal is dressed and dragged back to it. Something that would obviously take time. But in the cold of winter, time passes very quickly when there's an emergency, or an accident, that needs attention.

Half-supporting, half-carrying him, Jack led Cyril back through the snow. Twice, they stopped when Cyril seemed to sag.

"Can you see, Cyril? We're almost at the house." Jack kept encouraging his brother.

He also kept hoping and probably praying. He kept looking at Cyril to see if there was any change. All he saw was blood, some of it congealing, much of it oozing and trickling to the snow beneath them. He knew that none of this was good. His only relief was seeing that Cyril's left eye seemed to flutter open from time to time. He hoped it was a good sign.

Just as they got to the house, there was another scream. This time it was from Amelia. She'd been to the outhouse and noticed her brothers struggling back through the snow. Then she'd seen the red and assumed the worst.

"Mom! Cyril's been shot!" she screamed through the door, and then ran back out to look again. The sight of all that blood on Cyril's face and clothing triggered tears and emotions in Amelia and, through the sobs, the question, "What happened?"

Rose dashed outside to hear Jack's incomprehensible answer that the rifle had exploded. Together, she and Jack carried Cyril into the house and sat him on a bench beside the table.

"Well, at least that was a new and clean deer-hide mitt a few weeks ago," Rose commented, slowly coaxing Cyril to remove the mitt that had been a temporary dressing, so she could begin to assess the damage. Then she helped Cyril out of his jacket and began to issue orders to the other two.

"Amelia, get some water on to boil. Then fetch me the newest and cleanest sheet. We've got to make some bandages. And, oh yes, I'll need that box with my sewing things." She pointed with one hand, while slowly and gently probing the area around the wound on Cyril's right cheek. He whimpered, and instinctively tried to pull away from her touch.

"Jack, clear the things off the table and help me put him on it," Rose ordered next, as Cyril's jacket slid to the floor. It had absorbed quite a lot of the blood.

"Do you want me to make tea, Mom?" Amelia asked.

"No. Just clean, clear, boiling water. Put more wood on if you have to."

Jack helped with the firewood part. It was something he felt comfortable doing. He wondered about the sewing things, but decided it would be best not to ask.

"It's clean and it's a straight cut," Rose said softly, stroking Cyril's hair back and out of the way. "Your cheek bone may be broken, though." She continued looking down at her son for a reaction. "Did you feel anything inside your mouth?"

There was already a big bruise, and Cyril's right eye was beginning to swell shut. But he was able to blink and say, "I swallowed a lot of blood. But that seems to have stopped now. Is that good?"

Rose smiled and nodded. "You're already starting to heal,"

she said reassuringly. Then, to Amelia, "Get the basin ready with water as hot as you can bear. You and I need to get cleaned up for the next part, with lots of soap and water."

Cyril was looking at the roof of their house from a position he had never been in before. Jack, however, was looking with some concern at his mom, as she got out some fine thread, cut six or seven short pieces, and then looked for a needle.

"Now, Amelia," she said, "boil water in our soup ladle, too, and then put the threaded needle into the ladle, and keep the needle and thread in the boiling water for a minute. Okay?"

Amelia nodded.

Then Rose told her son exactly what she was going to do and what he would feel. She told him several times in a slow, methodical tone. Then, four times she repeated the painful task of threading, boiling, and suturing, until all that was left on the swollen side of Cyril's face was a trace of the gash that the bolt of the rifle had produced. A gash now pulled together by four painful stitches. She smiled down at Cyril's ashen face. He had accepted the painful procedure because, at the first push of the needle, he had settled into what she explained to Jack and Amelia was a deep sleep.

"It happens when people are hurt or injured," she explained through her own tears. "The body avoids further pain by going into a deep sleep, like fainting."

As Rose began to clean Cyril's face, she realized that he would require considerable care for the next few days. She listened to his slow breathing and looked for signs that color might be returning to his face. She also knew that the best place for him would be in his bed. But not stained and soiled, and covered in blood.

"Jack," Rose ordered, "take off his shoe-packs. Then bring in extra firewood and build up the fire. Amelia, fill the water pails and put them to heat on the stove. And," she continued, "when you've done that, the two of you go out and bring in that deer before some wolves find it."

"Is Cyril all right, Mom?" Amelia asked.

"Yes," Rose smiled firmly. "He'll wake up soon. I'll just clean him up and put him to bed. He'll need warmth and rest in order to heal. But you two need to look after that deer before it gets too dark."

In the quiet warmth of the little log house, Rose became mother to her little boy lying on the table. Her baby boy, who had tried to prove he was a man. She kept him warm with blankets as she gently removed his clothes and let them drop into the wash tub beside the stove. She smiled and wept, as she realized how much pain he had endured, and how he had tried not to show it. She hoped that in the process of it all, Amelia had been too busy with the medical things to notice that he had wet himself. She hoped that Cyril had not noticed and, if he had, that he might forgive her for looking after him, and putting him to bed in a clean union suit that seemed to have gotten too small for him.

Rose had put Cyril into bed, and had just added the last of the water from his sponge bath to his soaking clothes, when she heard him stir and moan. She rushed over to sit beside him.

"It hurts," he spluttered through clenched teeth. "Am I okay?"

"You are now," Rose smiled.

Cyril tried to look around, but one eye was closed and bandaged over, along with the cut. He seemed confused about what had happened. Rose could see him moving around under the blankets.

"Where's Jack and Amelia?" Cyril asked. "And how did I get here?" Then he grimaced in pain at having tried to talk, and the pain continued to burn on the right side of his face.

"I sent them away to look after the deer." Then, sensing that Cyril was probably asking about something else, she added, "Jack said he was the biggest buck we've ever seen around here."

But Cyril was thinking of other things. "You looked after me, didn't you?" he asked.

"I did what was needed," Rose said, leaning down to kiss her boy's forehead. "And now, I'll make us some tea. Sweet, the way you like it."

15

It took Jack and Amelia some time to get back to where the deer was. Amelia had a lot of questions. Jack decided to tell her what he could, but only as much as she really needed to know. He knew he was practicing his stories for when he'd really need to explain things.

"Dad will want to see this," Jack said. He'd pulled the Ross rifle out of the snow where it had landed. The bolt was back, the breech open, and the spent shell ejected. It looked almost normal. But Jack knew it wasn't. It couldn't be, not after what had happened. He remembered the warnings he'd heard. He leaned it against a tree. Amelia was staring down at the deer.

"It's just like a rabbit, only bigger," Jack explained. "You've helped Cyril and me with rabbits we snared, remember?"

"It's still warm," Amelia noted. "Is it really dead?"

"It's still warm because it's a big animal. And it really isn't all that cold out today." Jack reached down and grabbed a front leg. "You do the same with that hind leg." He pointed. "We'll roll it onto its back. It's too heavy to hang."

Jack and Cyril had helped in the field dressing of at least three or four big animals each year. The animal's antlers acted as props for the front end. Jack left Amelia in charge of the back part.

"Just spread the legs and pull them down as far as possible," Jack ordered. "Sit on them if you want, and don't look at what I have to do."

Amelia didn't look. But she could hear. And she knew what was happening. The smell of more than ten rabbits being gutted all at once wafted over her.

"Stand on one leg and lift the other one as high as you can," Jack ordered, and almost gagged as he opened his mouth. He'd cut and split the breastbone and, as the deer rolled, the offal began to fall out and sink into the snow because of its warmth.

Jack was sweating when he finally told Amelia to help him roll the deer a couple of times, to get clear of the guts and things, that they then covered with leaves and snow. Amelia pretended she was fine, and that she was just shivering because she was getting cold.

"Now comes the fun part," Jack said, trying to smile. "You get to pull his coat off. He's too big to drag back as is, so we'll just quarter him here and use the hide to drag back what we can manage. Okay?"

Amelia nodded. "But what should I do?" she asked.

"Just pull on this rope while I cut away the hide. Pull as hard as you can." Jack had skinned the front legs, attached one end of the rope to the hide of each leg, and looped the other end around Amelia's waist. "Pull!" he yelled again and again, while he separated the hide from the fat and carcass beneath.

A half-hour later, Amelia had pulled off the rubbery hide and Jack was busy with his knife and hatchet, quartering the deer. He placed each piece of the growing pile onto the hide.

It was well into darkness by the time they could smell the fire of their wood stove, and see the light glowing through the window of the house.

"This is the last part," Jack said. "Help me hang the meat in the shed, and then we'll stretch the hide and tack it to the outside of the shed."

Amelia helped without question or protest. She did not want to go into the house by herself. She was worried and afraid of what she might find. She suspected they'd been sent out to get the deer for reasons other than just to save it from wolves or whatever.

"Is he all right?" Amelia whimpered the question, as tears started to glisten in her eyes.

The curtain was back, and she could see Cyril propped up in the boys' bed. Then she ran and threw her arms around her mom.

"He was so still and white, and ..." Amelia's words tailed off as she sobbed and as Rose drew her to her side.

"He fainted because of the pain," Rose said as she stroked her daughter's hair. "He's still very sore but he's okay now. Come and see."

Amelia swiped away at her tears, her hands smelling like dead deer, as she walked with Rose over to her brother. "Hi ... you okay?" was all she could manage, as she looked down at the bandaged head, with one eye trying to smile back an answer.

"It's sore," Cyril wheezed through his clenched teeth.

"It probably broke, or severely bruised, his cheekbone," Rose said. "It will be very sore for him to open his mouth for a while."

"This here's what did it." Jack had come up behind them and was holding up the Ross rifle. He tapped the bolt that was still sticking out the way it wasn't supposed to.

"Is there blood on it?" Cyril managed to ask.

"It doesn't look like it."

Rose tried to smile and said, "I think his clothes got all the blood Cyril could spare. Now, come away. He needs rest. There's stew on the stove."

"Stew will taste better when that deer becomes part of it," Jack said. He tried to laugh and looked over to Cyril for a reaction.

"If he can't talk, then he can't laugh, silly," Amelia stated. She then added that she needed to wash her hands and get rid of the yucky deer smell.

16

Cyril's bandage was off the next day. Rose wanted to check for bleeding. She seemed pleased that there was only some slight drainage from around the sutures. "We'll leave the bandage off to let the air get at it. It only looks like a black eye and a big bruise," she said. "Let me know when you want to sit by the fire."

Cyril gingerly felt around the right side of his face. His right eye felt itchy, but it was swollen shut. "Mom, can I look at it in the mirror?" he wheezed through his teeth.

Rose brought the small mirror from the wall, and Amelia hovered in the background, as Cyril explored the damage done by the rifle. "It probably feels worse than it looks," Rose said. "The swelling should go down in a day or so."

"Does it hurt bad?" Amelia asked. "Do you want to play with the kittens? I could get them for you."

"Maybe later," Rose suggested. "And maybe you should go out, too. You could help Jack with some sawing."

Amelia didn't know whether she would like working with Jack. She knew he would want to be boss. "Why do I have to be down below in all the sawdust?" she asked, when Jack told her to pull on the bottom end of the saw.

"That's the easy part," he told her. "I have to be up here to steer the saw in a straight line. You don't even have to look at what you're doing. Just pull."

"I need a kerchief or something to keep the sawdust off me," Amelia insisted after her first feeble pull. She ran to the house and emerged looking like an old lady with a shawl around her head.

Jack laughed and shook his head. "Pull!" he yelled. "Just pull by hanging on the saw if you want to. I'll guide it and help by pushing as much as I can."

Unlike the crosscut, the rip saw was stiff enough to be pushed as well as pulled. After a hundred strokes, with Amelia's help, they were making progress. Enough so that, much to Amelia's relief, they had to stop to reposition the timber they were working on.

"Hah!" Amelia said, finally able to look up. "We are making progress. I really am helping."

"Well, help some more," Jack ordered. "We need to cut one board each day to keep up with our schedule."

He wasn't all that sure what the schedule was, or just how many boards they would need for the scow. It just seemed like something a boss would say. Two things he didn't say, however, were that he was surprised that, for being so small and inexperienced, Amelia had cut about as much as Cyril would have in the same amount of time, and that he was getting tired by the time their mom called them in for lunch.

"We cut half a board," Amelia announced with pride, shaking the sawdust off herself. "We'll finish it this afternoon, right, Jack?"

"Well, maybe. If I have time," he replied. "I want to set some snares, and there are a few more old traps Dad left behind. I may be able to add to our income here, close to the house."

"Maybe Amelia should be your assistant in that, too," Rose suggested.

Jack sighed as a way of stating his objections. But he didn't argue. He'd seen her looking in the direction of the bed where Cyril was sleeping again. He realized the dangers of being out alone in the wintertime, even if it was fairly close to the house. The extra traps were a new addition. They might have to go a bit farther out into the bush to set them.

17

By the time Malcolm came back from his own trap lines at midday a few days later, Cyril was able to look after himself again—although his meals were still of the liquid variety. It hurt to move his lower jaw, and his face still felt puffy from the bruising. But, as Amelia pointed out, the bruising did have interesting colors as it healed.

After he'd heard the story, seen the rifle, and looked at Cyril a second time, Malcolm told Jack to come out and help him stretch some pelts. He picked up the Ross rifle and brought it out with him. Rose didn't say anything, except for Amelia to stay in and help her with something for supper.

Jack knew the pelts were an excuse. But he didn't argue. He knew his dad would want to hear about the rifle incident from him alone.

"I didn't know that guns could do that," Jack began lamely, looking at the Ross rifle out by the shed.

"Anything a person can make can also break," Malcolm replied, sounding almost philosophical. "It just depends on how they're used, or who uses them."

Malcolm tried the bolt in the rifle and could feel the dark heat rising in the back of his head. It was the anger of having seen guns look like that during the war. It was also the memory of the damage those guns could do when not used properly, or as intended. But most of all, it was the anger from its having struck again so close to home.

"I showed Cyril how the rifle worked before we went out," Jack said.

"I showed you how to use it!" Malcolm roared. "You think you can teach someone with just one lesson? Soldiers couldn't learn after months of drills and training!" He held out the rifle so Jack could see the gaping breech, and the place where some cogs on the bolt had broken off.

"Dad?" Jack was trying to find the right words. "Dad, what can I do to fix it?"

"Fix it!?" Malcolm was shaking, trying to control his anger. "Fix what? This rifle? Your brother?"

Jack looked away. He wondered how far he would have to go to get away from the explosion that was happening. He wondered about thunder and how far it echoed from up in the mountains.

"You can't fix this rifle!" Malcolm yelled. "It's busted! The mechanism needs to be replaced!" He held the rifle at arm's length to show Jack. "And you can't fix Cyril! His face is busted! He'll have a scar to remind him for the rest of his life!"

Malcolm wanted to take the rifle and swing it hard against the side of the shed. He wanted to swing and hurl it into the Athabasca River. And, from the way he was feeling, he would probably have gotten it almost as far as that in that instant of rage.

But then he saw Jack's face. A boy, a young man, bewildered and tearful. Afraid of what was happening and what his life had become. It was a look and memory from decades before. The war had followed him home. He had brought it home with him.

At that moment, the door of the house opened. Another image of war appeared.

"Dad, it was my fault," Cyril pleaded.

There was only silence.

"Dad, I asked Jack to let me shoot. It's my fault."

Malcolm looked from one son to the other. From one memory to another. Memories old and new from which he could not escape.

"No," Jack said, "I let him. I thought it was all right. We even cleaned the rifle the night before, out here in the shed."

Malcolm looked down. Memories kept coming back. Long, cold nights at the front. The thunder of guns. The flash of explosions. The fear of those sleepless nights and of soldiers awaiting the punishment of the coming day. Of them fearfully, nervously doing what they could in the darkness of their imprisonment of war. And he had been one of them, praying, and promising that everything would be different if he made it through that night, and the next, and the next, and all the days and nights that might follow.

Malcolm looked away to the horizon and saw the sun of the late winter afternoon settling slowly down to the level of the trees. He was standing with his sons, the elusive future he once thought would never be his.

He looked at Cyril, now almost to his shoulders. Slowly Malcolm stretched out his right hand and, with the knuckle of his forefinger, stroked away the stream of tears flowing from his boy's left eye. Cyril didn't move. Perhaps it was defiance; perhaps it was him sensing that something far greater was happening.

Malcolm said, "You'd best wipe the other eye yourself. It looks mighty sore. And then you get into the house. Jack and I have some pelts to stretch before it gets too dark."

There were about twenty pelts, mostly small. All of them the kind that could be pulled easily over the drying boards, their feet tacked so they would stay in place. They worked together. Malcolm used his knife to clean off some of the fat still adhering to the pelts. Jack found the right size board for each and tacked the pelt in place.

They worked together in silence until Jack said, "I've set some more of your old traps and our usual snares close to the house." He was testing to see what he could say, or maybe to find out what his dad was thinking.

After a while Malcolm said, "I noticed some of the old traps weren't in the shed. Whatever you can do here, aside from sawing boards, will be a help in the spring, or next summer."

The meal afterward was quiet. Everyone pretended to be hungry for the stew that Rose and Amelia had prepared.

Malcolm finally broke the silence. "I see from the calendar that the next time I come back from the trap lines, it will probably be Christmas."

Amelia and Cyril looked at each other on hearing that peculiar announcement, but decided not to ask any further. They'd heard about Christmas in one of the stories in a reader, but had never thought that such a thing could apply to them out in the bush, away from towns and people.

That night, Jack heard the other strange thing—quiet whispering coming from behind the curtain in the direction of his parents' bed.

"Where are we on this thing, anyway?" Jack asked his mom the next morning. He was looking intently at the calendar, all curled up at the corners from being re-cycled for the last three years.

Cyril was near the stove, teasing one of the kittens. Amelia was outside with the rest of the cats, as she had already started to call them.

Rose understood Jack's question, but Malcolm hadn't said anything else by way of explanation. And he had left in the cold darkness of early morning. Probably to avoid any questions.

"We're at the beginning of December, I think," Rose answered, pulling in behind Jack and tracing her fingers over the numbers.

The days hadn't mattered all that much before. And where they lived, there were no train whistles, no church bells, or any social schedule by which to gauge the progress of the year. Only nature's seasons.

Then Rose said, almost brightly, "Your dad said he'd be home in three weeks. So, let's just imagine that this is December second. It's a Monday." She found a pencil to circle that date. "We can keep track from today onward," Rose said, standing back and admiring what she had done.

They had a schedule. They had joined the world of clocks and calendars.

"Is Christmas the red number?" Cyril asked, sensing the

magnitude of the situation. Then he continued, "That means there should be at least twenty boards added to our lumber pile by then."

"Your other eye will have to be really open before you can work on that," Jack told him. "Although Amelia seems to be able to do about as much as you."

Cyril appealed to his mom for medical advice. "Do you think my eye is healing fast enough?" he asked.

"You'll see for yourself," Rose answered, and then almost laughed at the realization that she had made a joke.

Things did seem different after that. It wasn't just that Christmas was coming, either. There were a lot of things that suddenly became important. They had a future. They had things to do aside from the routine of just living from day to day and season to season.

18

Jack took control of the lumber yard when the weather permitted—although being boss wasn't easy. Cyril was anxious to get back to work, but Amelia insisted that she had earned a spot on the workforce with the rip saw. She'd also stopped asking about shelves and a new bed.

Rose's medical opinion about Cyril's wound held sway for a while. "It's broken," she told him. "I saw it. Any pressure or bump will delay the healing."

"And besides," Jack added, "you could get sawdust in your eye."

It was mid-morning. They were having a tea break. They were in the thick of a December that had not let up with either snow or cold. All the new snow on the roof of their house at times made it look like a giant mushroom.

"I could try working on the top end of the saw," Cyril persisted. "You could show me how, Jack. And that way, all three of us could be working." He looked over to Amelia for support.

"And what would I do?" Rose almost laughed.

"Well, the lumber and the logs do keep getting covered with snow," Jack hinted.

That seemed to work. Rose used the words "co-operation" and "rotation" as the four of them spelled each other off in the various positions and jobs around the saw pit, once Cyril had mastered guiding the saw from above. The only times there were only three of them working at sawing was when Jack went to check his traps, or when Rose decided that something needed to be done about meals.

A few days before the big red-numbered day on the calendar called Christmas, they were down to a few small spruce logs and all of the bigger, longer ones. Jack had told them they would be left until last, once they had developed enough skill.

"Dad should be home tomorrow, or the day after, shouldn't he?" Jack asked at supper.

"And then it's Christmas!" Amelia shouted, startling Harley and Samantha, as she'd named the orange kitten.

"Yes," Rose stated slowly, looking over at Jack. He looked like he might have more to say.

"I was thinking that maybe I should go out and meet him," Jack said. Then, gaining courage, "The snow's deep. He'll be carrying some bales of fur. I would be breaking trail for him and helping."

"You don't know the trail," Rose said flatly. "And you shouldn't be out there on your own. It's not safe."

As soon as she had said those things, however, Cyril joined in on the argument. "I could go, too," he smiled. "I've been snowshoeing for years, Mom."

"The trail's along the river," Jack stated. "I went hunting that way with Dad. He said that we were more than halfway to his trap lines. Besides, we probably won't even get a mile or so before we meet up with him."

"And if you don't?" Rose shot back. "How far is it to his cabin?"

"Just over ten miles, I think."

"Dad usually walks it in half a day," Cyril added. "Even with a full pack."

Rose played her final card as a protective mother. "But you don't have a gun. And your dad did say there were more wolves and coyotes this year."

"Mom," Jack said, with a certain degree of authority, "there'll be two of us. We'll be making lots of noise. Besides, they like to hunt at night. We'll leave first thing in the morning." He realized that the last part sounded like he was in command, so he added, "Okay?"

Cyril nodded in the background.

Amelia added, "Maybe we could do something special while they're gone," and joined in on the nodding.

The next day promised to be clear and cold. The morning rush to the outhouse was their weather report. There were still stars in the sky when they looked up.

The sun was starting to shine on their backs a short while later, when Jack and Cyril began their slow trek through the snow that had covered the trail in the last few weeks. Jack knew they would not travel as fast as their dad, but they would try. They also knew that it would be at least noon before there would be any chance of meeting up with him. The snow was deep and heavy.

"It's this way," Jack told Cyril, when they got down to near the small river.

They weren't the only ones to follow the path of least resistance, though. The hollow depressions of a moose from a few days before showed the way for the next half-mile or so.

"How do you know it's a moose?" Cyril asked.

"Big prints, but in a straight line, like a deer," Jack told him. "He's looking for a swampy area for something to forage on."

"Has Dad seen them up at the cabin?"

"I don't know. He hasn't said, has he?"

"He never says very much," Cyril replied. "Did he ever talk to you about the rifle we busted?"

"No. Not really. Like you said, he doesn't say very much." The snow was almost knee deep, even with their snowshoes. "It's your turn to lead and break trail," Jack ordered.

Cyril reluctantly forged ahead. His shorter legs made things a lot harder for him. It certainly made it harder for him to talk.

The sun had gotten as high as it was going to get. It hardly made it to the height of the trees before starting to settle back down to earth. Jack tried to remember if there had been a full moon the night before. He wasn't worried. He just wanted to know, and he was angry with himself for not having checked.

"Mom gave us some biscuits. We might as well take a break and eat them now."

"I thought you were never going to stop," Cyril whistled. "This is hard work."

"You get used to it on the trap lines," Jack told him. Then he added, "Maybe you should start coming with me. I could teach you a few things."

"Yeah, like you did with the rifle. Shit, my cheek's throbbing worse with all this walking."

They were almost five miles from home. Jack figured this was not the time nor the place for an argument. They were hot and sweaty from lifting their snowshoes through the weight of all the new snow. They munched on their biscuits in silence.

"Are we going all the way to Dad's cabin?" Cyril asked, when they started out again. "It's ten miles. What if he didn't start out for the house today?"

"We'll go for a while longer," Jack said. "We'll have a packed trail for the way back. It'll be easier for us. And Dad will appreciate the easier walking on it, too."

About an hour later, they stopped again. It had been a day of hard work. And the trail wasn't straight or flat. It simply followed the path of least resistance, as it vaguely meandered along beside the little river that gurgled beside them from time to time.

"How much farther?" Cyril asked again.

"How should I know? I've never been to Dad's trapping cabin."

"Then how do you know how long it will take for us to get there?"

It was a simple question, highlighting a simple fact. It would soon be getting dark, and the signs of the trail, such as they were, would be harder to follow.

"I don't know! We don't know!" Jack sounded frustrated at the dilemma. They could flounder on and hope to get to the cabin, maybe. Or they could turn tail and head back to the house. At least the trail back would be packed and easy to follow, even at night.

Jack was tired. Without saying anything else, he turned around, pushed past Cyril, and forged ahead on the way back. He knew it was the right decision, even though he was not happy making it. "Come on!"

The moon came up almost as soon as the sun went down. Not full, but it would give some light. It would be a cold, clear night. Jack knew they'd have to maintain a steady pace just to stay warm. What he didn't know, or couldn't figure out, was why they had not reached the cabin or their dad. Less than a mile farther, they found out.

"Shit! There's someone else on the trail," Cyril wheezed. He was in the lead at this point, and confused. They were both staring at an intersection to their trail.

"It's Dad," Jack said, knowing he'd be in trouble again. "Look at the arrow in the snow. He knows we've been here."

"But he didn't wait for us. He's heading to the house." Then Cyril asked a more obvious question. "How did we miss him?"

Jack didn't answer. But what he did say led them to making another very serious decision. "He's not alone. Look." He pointed to several pairs of big tracks.

"Shit ..." Cyril whispered it slowly this time. "Wolves? And they're following Dad, aren't they? What will we do?"

Jack knew he couldn't be wrong this time. "We could try to go to Dad's cabin and hole up. But we don't know how long that might take us. And there could be more wolves. Or we could try to head for home and hope to catch up with Dad."

"And the wolves," Cyril said ominously, his teeth chattering.

"When we find one, we'll find the other." Jack had made his decision. "Those animals are probably following the scent of his pelts. That's what they're interested in."

Without waiting for any comment or argument, Jack set off at a rapid pace. He knew Cyril had no choice but to follow and keep up. They could move a lot faster over a trail that had now been packed by three people. And at least as many big animals.

Jack stopped at the top of every rise. Not to rest but to listen.

"With the load of his pack, and with the coldness of the trail, we might be able to hear his snowshoes somewhere up ahead," Jack whispered back to Cyril, as the two of them stopped for the third time.

Cyril was doubled over, his hands resting on his knees, forcing the cold air in and out of his burning lungs. "And that means," he wheezed, "that those wolves will also hear us."

"No," Jack assured him. "Once they're on the trail of something, they stay on it."

"Listen!" But Cyril hardly needed to say it. It was the unmistakable "Paff!" sound of their Cooey .22 off in the distance.

They heard it pierce the moonlit winter air six times. About ten seconds between each shot.

"Shit!" Cyril exclaimed. He couldn't help using that word again because of the implications. "Six wolves? A whole pack?"

"No," Jack said more objectively, teaching his little brother. "It's only our .22. One shot to hit them, and one more to kill them. Three wolves. Look at their tracks." He pointed to the shadowy prints on the trail ahead. Then, taking command once again, "Come on. Dad'll need us."

Jack and Cyril shuffled along as fast as they could. The trail was slightly downhill and, with the moonlight helping to show the way, they were soon up to where their dad was already skinning out the first of the wolves. Jack didn't expect a greeting.

Malcolm explained that he'd killed the wolves in that spot for a reason. "I knew you'd catch up to me sooner or later. I didn't want them to get wind of you and maybe double back. They're unpredictable that way. You can help with skinning them. Easier than dragging them back to the house."

"Good size and nice pelts, aren't they?" Jack said, more by way of conversation than anything else, as he and Cyril stretched out each animal, while their dad used his knife and his skill to skin them.

"Lot of wolves this year," Malcolm acknowledged. "Some coyotes, too." Then he repeated something he'd overheard in Hinton in the summer. "They say they might fetch a good price at the Edmonton auction."

"How come we missed you on the trail, Dad?" Cyril wanted to know.

"You were on my old river trail. It goes by some falls near the cabin. It's too hard breaking trail with a heavy load."

Jack nodded. "That's why we came out. I knew the snow would be deep. It was slow going."

Cyril was already rolling up the wolf pelts. "We can help carry," he volunteered.

Malcolm disposed of the wolf carcasses beside the trail. "The house isn't far now," he said, looking up at the moon. "Jack, you carry the rifle and a bale of pelts on this tumpline. Cyril, you bring up the rear with those wolf pelts. It'll make it easier for other wolves to track us."

The boys couldn't tell whether or not their dad was smiling when he said that. Both of them kept up, whatever the load, or the distance back to the house.

"Is it Christmas tomorrow?" was the first thing Amelia asked when the door opened.

"I heard a gun a while back," Rose said.

"A Christmas bonus," Malcolm said wryly. But, in the house, and by the light of the lamp, both Jack and Cyril could see that this time, he was smiling through his gray and bushy beard.

"Christmas," Malcolm decreed, looking at the calendar later that evening, "will be in two days. The day after tomorrow. I can't leave the trap lines for too long."

19

The next day was a day of preparation. Rose and Amelia seemed to be busy with the little stove and a lot of new things being cooked. Malcolm was busy outside, cleaning and stretching pelts. He said he wanted to do those things himself.

"Well," Jack stated, once the morning seemed to be underway, "I've got a trap line to check. Cyril, do you want to come?"

That suggestion was as odd as all the other things going on around the Whyte household in the middle of winter. The trap line near the house had been Jack's personal domain, just like his lookout by the river, from which he had watched the eagles in the summers. Only the rabbit snares closer to the house had been a combined effort by the two boys. Something they had done for years to add meat to the stew pot, and to practice skinning and looking after furs.

For the second day in a row, Jack and Cyril tied on their snowshoes and set off for the dense woods. It had turned mild, and a trace of new snow muffled their progress along Jack's trapping trail. Jack had cleaned up and experimented with some of the rusty traps that his dad had let him have the winter before, and now he had twenty. His trapping had become more than just experimenting. He could imagine that by the end of winter, he might have as many as a hundred mink or weasel pelts to add to the family's income.

After the first loop of about half the traps, the boys took a rest. Cyril stroked the fur of one of the three mink they'd taken so far.

"Something's happening with Dad." Jack just came right out and said what was on his mind. It had been his reason for bringing Cyril along.

"Yeah, he's nice." Cyril felt his cheek. Then he added, "No beatings and no yelling. I'd expected more than what we got when we busted the rifle."

"Well, he did sort of yell at me a bit. Like I should have known better." Jack looked over through the trees, making sure that they really were alone, but making it look like he was checking on the weather. Then he looked at Cyril, gauging his reaction. "But all of this, this last year, is strange. It's like he's planning something."

"Yeah, he wants us to leave the bush." Cyril almost laughed at what had seemed so obvious. "He wants us to move to Edmonton.

It's supposed to be a hundred times bigger than Hinton or Brûlé." To Cyril, that was like the promise of going to the biggest general store in the world, and with counters full of candy.

"But why?" Jack persisted. "And why did we come out here in the first place?"

"Depression, I guess," Cyril answered, as if that covered everything.

"But Dad said Edmonton," Jack stated. "Why would we move to a big city? Why not to Whitecourt? Wasn't that where Mom and Dad were from?"

"Do we still have relatives there?" Cyril asked. "Mom never talks about them. Not to me, anyway. Maybe to Amelia."

"Maybe they left, too. Our relatives from Whitecourt, I mean." Jack wasn't sure that Cyril understood what he was trying to say. Maybe you had to be a man to think like a man. Jack wondered if Cyril would always seem like a boy to him—the little brother he had to look after.

They were both getting cold. The damp raw wind indicated there woud be a snowstorm soon.

"Let's check the other traps," Jack suggested. "If there aren't too many, we'll wait until we get home before we skin them."

Cyril was already on his feet, on the trail, and looking back. "This way?" he asked.

Jack nodded. "Yeah." Having said what he had, he began

to wonder how accurate his observations of their dad had been. The load on his mind had not become any lighter by sharing it. Not yet, anyway.

Jack wished it was summer. Sitting up on the bluffs at his special spot, he had always found it so easy to understand things while watching his eagles. Finding answers to things with other people always seemed so difficult. Maybe it was because the eagles didn't talk. They just made you look up and dream.

By the time Jack and Cyril headed home, the snow had started. They'd added two more mink and a marten to their day's haul.

"You'll have no trouble making more stretchers for the extra pelts you're bringing in," Malcolm said, nodding to the boards the boys had been sawing and stockpiling. He'd spent the day dealing with pelts and furs.

Jack nodded his response. He and Cyril had also talked about the kinds of things they might make out of the extra boards once the scow was built.

They continued working in silence until dark and the call to supper.

Christmas Eve, or anything associated with Christmas, was foreign to the Whyte children. It was something else they had left behind in Brûlé, swallowed up by the Depression. It was an extravagance they could not afford, or to which they no longer had access. Christmas was something done in churches and by people. Christmas was the sort of thing you had to be reminded of by a calendar.

When Malcolm Whyte had circled that red number on the last set of squares labeled December, Christmas became real again. It was an event to be anticipated and for which they all, to varying degrees, prepared.

On Christmas Eve, after a supper of grouse, and boiled pudding for dessert, the boys hung cedar boughs around the house to make it smell nice. And then, in the glow of the coal oil lamp, Rose read the Christmas story from the small black Bible the church had given them when she and Malcolm had been married. The front page had their names and dates, and on the next page, Rose had added the full names of Jack, Cyril, and Amelia, and when and where they had been born.

It was still dark on Christmas morning, when Jack and Cyril raced through their routines at the outhouse and with the wood pile. The snow was beginning to let up, but the air still felt mild for a winter day.

"What happens on a Christmas morning?" Cyril asked his older brother who, he assumed, would have some memories about such things.

"It used to be Santa Claus and presents, from what I remember," Jack said. "At least, it used to be for the little kids."

Then he shrugged. "But we're way off in the bush. It hasn't ever been a Santa Claus kind of place."

"Mom did a lot of cooking, though, didn't she," Cyril stated. "That should make things kind of special."

Something special wafted through the door as soon as they opened it, with their arms full of the day's supply of firewood.

"Pancakes!" Amelia announced. "And with special preserves. It took us a whole day to pick berries to make this jam. And there's other stuff for later. But that's a surprise."

Near the end of their pancake breakfast, Malcolm excused himself. Rose smiled mysteriously. She knew that his idea about Christmas had had its origins during the summer. Malcolm came back shortly, looking a bit like Santa Claus. At least, he had his bushy beard, which was now mostly gray, and he had a sack.

"It's a good thing those bobcats of Amelia's like living out in the shed, and like hunting mice," he said, adding to the mystery of the event.

"What is it?" was the loud and demanding question of all three Whyte children. Children, because in that instant, they all really were children. Even Jack. And they all had grins of anticipation to prove it.

"This," Malcolm said, with as much ceremony and fanfare as the little house had ever seen, "this is for all of us." He pulled out a tin and handed it to Rose and Amelia.

"Dried fruit," Rose said, almost reverently. "Apricots, raisins, and prunes."

"And what are these?" Amelia asked, holding up a ring of wrinkled things held together with a wooden-looking lace of some sort.

"Figs," Malcolm explained. "The man at the store said they came all the way from Greece."

The boys were mystified. Rose said, "We haven't had fruit of any kind for years. Not since we moved out here." Then, in response to Amelia's pleading gaze, she said, "You can each have five raisins to see if you like them."

"It's like candy if you suck on them one at a time," Cyril commented after experimenting.

Malcolm smiled and nodded. Then he dove back into his sack. "For the two of you," he said, handing Rose and Amelia a brown paper package.

Rose held the package while Amelia pulled on the twine to untie the knot.

"The wife at the Hinton store helped. She said there's enough there to make two dresses," Malcolm said, as Rose and Amelia unfolded some printed calico cloth. "There's also enough buttons and things."

The boys looked on, not knowing what to say, but obviously hoping that the Santa Claus sack might hold something for them, too. They held their breath, as Malcolm dove back in and fished around in the bottom of the burlap bag.

"Here," he said, thrusting another brown paper package their way.

They cut the twine and unfolded the wrapping as if it were a competition.

"Real pants! Jeans," Jack said, examining the blue denim.

"And belts!" Cyril added, retrieving the leather contraptions from where they had landed on the floor.

"Well," Malcolm said, "you can't go into town next summer in old worn-out coveralls, can you?"

There was a flurry of arms and legs, as Jack and Cyril both stepped into the first real pants either of them could remember. They rolled up the cuffs, cinched up the belts, and proclaimed that in a few months, they would fit perfectly.

They all said a big thank you to Santa.

Amelia said, "But what did you get, Dad?"

"A lot of pleasure," Malcolm said, and smiled at all of them. "A lot of pleasure."

The children reverted to being exactly that—children—and acted like they were years younger than they were. On a mild Christmas Day, they made snowmen, had snowball fights, and tried to pack down some snow to make it icy enough for a long slide. At times, it sounded like their numbers had multiplied.

Malcolm watched for a while. Hearing their laughter made him wonder if such things could be maintained for a whole year. He looked at the sky and hoped for a cold day the next morning, to make his walk back to the trap lines a little easier.

There was one more surprise in the burlap sack. After a dinner of venison and some of the dried fruit, boiled in a spicy syrup to make it look like the fruit it might at one time have been, Malcolm produced a small box that contained little black wooden tiles with dots, called dominoes.

They spent the evening learning how to play that game, arguing about the rules, and laughing when someone was lucky enough to win.

They'd already read the Christmas story the night before and, even though Amelia said she'd like to hear it again, Rose read them something called the chapter about love. She said that the minister had read it at their wedding. She'd kept a bookmark in just that spot. On it she'd written, "Charity never faileth— Love never ends."

The next morning, Malcolm quietly slipped away while it was still dark. It was cold, as he had wanted.

20

It was winter. It was cold and white, and often the smoke from the chimney went straight up, indicating just how cold January and February could be in the foothills of the Rocky Mountains in northern Alberta. Jack and Cyril were glad to be working at the logs most days. The sawing kept them warm and occupied. Filing the saw gave them an excuse to sit close to the fire every second evening. The evening in between was used to play the domino game. Rose said they would wear out the tiles before winter was over. Although she laughed when she said it.

Jack's longer trap lines and snares also became a job for both boys. It helped lighten the load if Cyril was along to carry things. It also made Rose more confident about their safety. There were more wolves and coyotes, and their only gun was with Malcolm at his trap lines.

Out on their trap lines, Jack and Cyril could talk privately—something that had never seemed all that important before. They were boys; they were brothers. Growing up, they had talked, fought, and played like other boys. But things change when you get older.

"I heard Dad say I could have been free," Jack told Cyril.

They were near the end of the first big loop on Jack's trap line. They'd just pulled a mink out of a trap, baited it, and reset it.

Cyril looked at the trap, the mink, and then at Jack. "What are you talking about?" he asked, not understanding what Jack might have had in common with a dead mink, or what their dad might have been talking about.

"No, nothing about traps," Jack frowned and looked serious. "Although, I guess I felt kind of trapped and was trying to get untangled and away from it all."

"Is this about last summer when you ran away?" Cyril could understand that. He was a boy. He'd run away more than once. Those were the times when he'd had the biggest beatings. He could still hear the smack of the belt, and feel it, too.

"Did Dad beat you last summer for running away? I know he was pretty mad when he went to look for you. You took his canoe. But you had a broken arm, didn't you?"

"No!" Jack said, cutting him off. "It's not as simple as that." He wondered if he could put into words what he was thinking. Maybe Cyril was still too much of a boy.

They were walking to the next trap. Walking slowly enough

so they could talk and still hear one another. At a bend in the trail, Jack said, "Dad almost drowned when he came for me. You know, when there was that big flood?"

"Shit." Cyril said it slowly. It always seemed to be the most significant word he used for anything important. "You never told us that! We all thought that your broken arm was the big thing. That, and the flood."

"Just shut up and listen. And don't talk about this to Mom." Jack had stopped and turned to face Cyril. It was all or nothing. He'd already said something; he had to continue. "Dad told me that if he'd drowned or died ..." Jack paused. "Then I would have been free. He wouldn't have been able to force me to come back here."

"Shit, what happened, anyway?" Cyril's eyes were wide at hearing such a story, such a secret. "Did you have to throw a rope out to him?"

"No! It was the big canoe. He got tangled in the bowline. The water was rising. Shit! All that doesn't matter! He nearly drowned. Okay?" Jack was shouting as he remembered it all. He was remembering the feeling of nearly drowning himself, and he could not put those memories into words so Cyril might understand. There was too much to describe. Cyril couldn't understand. He hadn't been there.

Jack was crying with exasperation and the memory of it. But most of all, he was crying because he had to share the biggest secret of his life. And, in telling it, break the bond of knowing that it had existed between his father and him alone.

He breathed deeply. "I think Dad wanted to die," Jack sad quietly. "I think that at times he may still want to die because, when he dies, then we'll all be free. You know, the rest of us."

Cyril was crying now, too. But in disbelief. He looked down at the trapped, the dead, the frozen mink he had been carrying. "How do you die?" he asked slowly.

"You have an accident, I guess. Or an accident happens to you."

"You mean, like with me and the rifle?" Cyril wondered out loud, wiping at his eyes and remembering. "Is that why Dad was mad about the rifle?"

"I don't know. I think he was mad that you got hurt. Or maybe he was mad at the rifle. He told me once that they didn't work too good in the war. Soldiers got hurt with them when they weren't careful."

Jack was starting to walk on. Walking was like watching the eagles. It helped him think. He wondered if he should have told Cyril any of this. It had always been his secret. His and his dad's.

"Dad can't have an accident. Not this winter," Cyril exclaimed, like he'd just solved a puzzle. "He wants to build a scow. And we can't do that until the spring, when it's warm and his trapping's done."

Jack was almost pleased that Cyril had said that. It meant he was thinking about things, too. "You're right. He wants to build a scow for the river, and for us to go to Edmonton," Jack answered. "But I don't think he wants to come with us. I don't think he really likes people. I think he watched too many of them die in the war. I think ..."

And here Jack stopped again and looked back at Cyril. "I think he wishes he had died in the war, too."

"But he never talks about being in the war." Cyril looked baffled.

"Maybe not. But that doesn't keep him from remembering, and then thinking about it. I think he has dreams about it."

"I dreamed about wolves chasing me and trying to eat me," Cyril said. "But that was when I was little."

"This is different. I think his dreams really hurt him."

Jack didn't say any more. They were almost back at the house. Even just smelling the wood smoke and seeing it in the distance made him afraid they might be overheard.

"Does Mom know any of this?" Cyril asked.

Jack stopped and looked down at his little brother. "No. And we can't tell her. She seems to be happy with what's happening. You know, with Christmas and all? And then building the scow in the spring? She and Amelia have been working on dresses."

Jack left it at that. He wondered if he'd maybe said too much.

Wondered if he might have made things worse. Sometimes sharing a secret can do that.

"This is between the two of us," Jack hissed at his brother. He'd stopped at the edge of the clearing to make sure Cyril understood. "I need to think some more about all of this. But if you talk, things could all fall apart."

Cyril nodded obediently. Under his breath he said, "Shit," again as he fell into step behind Jack.

21

Jack and Cyril were working on the "big, big" logs, as they called them, when the longer, brighter days of winter started to arrive. Those were the days when, if you worked hard enough, and it wasn't too windy, you could soon be down to your shirt sleeves.

Malcolm had told the boys to wait until he was home from his trapping, and he would show them how to set up the block and tackle so they could slide and hoist the big spruce logs into place for sawing. Rose and Amelia were also outside for that event. Rose assumed that some extra help might be needed after Malcolm had gone back up to his trap lines again.

Those big logs needed to be sawn into thicker, wider boards for the bottom of the scow. Malcolm had stayed back an extra day, just to help with squaring off one side of the first log. The boys knew he also needed to make some calculations.

"We need to figure out how wide those boards will be." Malcolm said, scribing a square outline on the end of a big log.

"If they're all about the same size, we'll need ten or twelve of them for the bottom of the thing."

Cyril whistled at that order for lumber. Jack just nodded his head. He'd already done some checking for himself.

"Do we have enough time to saw all those boards and then build the thing?" Jack asked.

Malcolm half-snorted, half-laughed. "I remember them building a few scows at Whitecourt," he said. "Always in the spring when there was little else to do. A crew of four or five men could build one in a week."

"Once all the boards were cut, right?" Cyril asked.

Malcolm nodded. "Their boards came from the mill," he said. "But not much better than these." He almost laughed again, but instead, it turned into a long spell of coughing.

Rose had overheard their conversation. She smiled at seeing them working so well together. And she smiled at what the project was leading up to. She pulled Amelia back into the house with her. It all seemed like a good reason to cook something special. There were still some raisins left from Christmas.

That evening, Malcolm became the boys' teacher, unlike the other evenings when their schooling fell to Rose. He asked for one of their scribblers and turned to the last page. "This is what you're cutting those boards for," he said, as he began to sketch a plan for their family scow.

"It's just a box," Amelia said, squeezing in and looking over her brothers' shoulders.

Jack and Cyril shushed her, as they asked questions of their own, and wondered how things would hold together.

"Those boards are like ribs," Malcolm said, drawing an arrow and adding another label. "They hold everything together, once the nails are clinched. And the front needs to be sloped to help it get over rocks and sand bars and things." He cleared his throat and continued to add details and drawings of special sections.

"But what keeps the water out?" Cyril wondered. "We can't stretch canvas over it like a canoe or use birch-bark patches."

"Remember that big bag of light stuff?" Malcolm asked. "It's full of coils of oakum. It gets forced into the cracks between the boards and then covered with tar."

"Like the stuff you've got for the roof?" Jack asked.

Malcolm laughed and coughed again. "Except," he said conspiratorially, "we won't need it for this roof anymore after this spring. It can leak all it wants."

It was a long evening and a short night. Malcolm wanted to be gone before any of the others were up. He was stoking the fire before he left, trying to be quiet, when Rose appeared beside him.

"It sounded like you were getting a cold last night," she said, handing him a small package. "There are a few figs from the dried fruit from Christmas. My mother used to say that figs were a cure for a cough or cold."

As Malcolm reached out to take them, Rose reached in and hugged him. It was an unusual gesture at that time of day, or for any other time of day, for that matter. She wanted to say something. To maybe thank him for working with the boys, and also for helping them to find their way. She hoped that her one-sided embrace would say more than words.

A few minutes later, Malcolm had put on his snowshoes, hoisted his pack, and disappeared into what was left of the shadows of the night, and what was still left of winter.

22

This was the first time Rose had worried about Malcolm leaving for his trap lines. For the seven winters they had already been there, the trap lines had been his job and his family's means of support. And, even during the Depression, each year had been better than the last.

But now, this year had been one of transition. It wasn't simply the reality of Jack asserting his independence and proving that he was no longer a boy. It was how he had done it or, rather, how he had come back. Jack wasn't defeated or beaten into boyhood obedience. If anything, he had become more like his father.

Rose looked out at her boys doing men's work with that big saw, day after day. They were working together. Encouraging each other under Jack's leadership. They had left Brûlé as little boys and floated down the Athabasca to this place, where time and chance had transformed them.

"Mom?" Cyril yelled from on top of the saw pit, as he took

a turn in directing the blade. "Do you want us to cut you some boards for anything?"

He was grinning with a look of accomplishment. Jack had counted and re-counted their stacks of boards. They were on the last one they would need for the scow, and there were two more spruce logs that could be sawn up for something.

Rose and Amelia had both turned to look from where they were propping up the clothesline. Today, things were actually flapping in the breeze. In the sunshine promise of spring, laundry no longer froze into boards.

"No!" Rose yelled back. "But you could always cut up some extra boards as spares, or possibly for boxes to store things in on the scow. You know, to keep things from rolling around?"

She left it as a question so they could think about it and make a decision. She knew they were anxious to get on with something else. The warmer weather had already made them bring in their traps and snares. Jack had muttered something about the coats of the animals already starting to change.

Those changes also meant that Malcolm would soon be coming in for the last time. It wasn't a routine but, in the evenings, they had each begun to look toward the hole in the bush and the trail coming down from his trapping cabin. Malcolm's final return would mark the beginning of the end of their life along the Athabasca.

23

The final two logs, a small one and a large one, both with flaws or noticeable bends in them, had been sawn into boards and set aside as extras. Jack and Cyril had worked into the evenings to do this. Probably, as Rose surmised, so they could get a better look up into the bush for their dad.

It was already days since they had anticipated Malcolm's return. A mild Chinook had passed, and the snow had already settled around their little house—a possible reason why Malcolm might not have ventured out on a soft and slushy trail with heavy packs. But now it was cold again. The trail was hard.

"Maybe Cyril and I should go up there to help him," Jack said one evening. Although it wasn't really said as a possibility, but rather as a decision already made.

"Yeah," Cyril added. "He's brought in one or two bales every time he's come back, but there's also a lot of other stuff to carry."

Rose nodded. Without saying it, the boys had expressed all

of their worries. She made some biscuits for them to take on the trail. The three children played dominoes. There were no shouts of victory or complaints about cheating.

Jack and Cyril tied on their snowshoes the next morning. The trail close to the house was hard enough to walk on without them, but they knew there could still be a lot of deep snow left in the bush. The sun was just coming up and beginning to shine on their backs as they left.

"He's probably wondering why we took so long." Cyril tried to sound cheerful, when he and Jack stopped for their first break later that morning. Jack had called it because he figured they were about halfway. They were both chewing on a biscuit and some dried meat.

Cyril then asked the obvious question they had all been thinking about, but which nobody had put into words. "You don't think something's happened for Dad to take this long, do you?"

"Nothing's ever happened before. Why should anything happen now?" Jack sounded angry. Probably because, deep down, he was. Changing, going back, was not something that Malcolm Whyte had wanted to do. Jack had been able to figure that much out. It was something that he wanted for his family, but not for himself. He could imagine his dad deliberately taking his time because he wanted to avoid change. Maybe he was even afraid of it.

"Come on," Jack ordered Cyril. "He said there were more wolves and coyotes this year. He probably needs help with the heavier work. He also set some bigger traps farther away to try to keep any wolves from raiding his other traps."

"You mean, more distance, more time, and more work. Right?" Cyril chewed on some salty dried meat as he ran to catch up.

Jack was relieved when they finally saw smoke rising from the stovepipe on the trapping cabin—although he didn't tell Cyril that. He'd never seen the cabin before. It looked hardly bigger than a small shed, like the one at the house, and a lot lower.

"Hello! Dad!" Jack yelled from a distance, not wanting their arrival to be too much of a surprise.

It wasn't. "What kept you?" were Malcolm's words of greeting. "There's more here than I can manage by myself. Too many coyotes this winter." He coughed to clear his throat.

He was still sitting on his small bunk. He hadn't come out as his boys had untied their snowshoes, banged them together to knock the snow off, and stuck them into the snow near the door. It took Jack and Cyril some time to adjust to the dim light after they came in. The only light came through some translucent animal gut stretched over a small hole in the door. The door itself closed a small opening and hung on rawhide hinges. The door wall could be covered on the inside by a big hide that rolled down to keep out some of the winds and drafts.

"We've come to give you a hand, if you need it," Jack said haltingly, not knowing what to say or what to ask. He and Cyril were still both in the doorway, waiting for their father to give them some indication of what was needed or expected.

"We finished sawing all the logs," Cyril said. And, not receiving any response, he added, "When do we start building the scow?"

After a while Malcolm said, "That's a good job for the spring, once the ground has dried. It's not nice to work in the mud."

"We could spread some sawdust," Cyril began.

But Jack cut him off. "It's too late to start back now, isn't it? What can we do?"

Malcolm looked up at his boys. "I've gotten behind," he confessed, waving a beaver pelt he'd been working on, stretching it over its circular frame. "I've cleared out most of the traps but didn't reset them. You boys could check the lines again and bring in the traps. At least, as many as you can handle. It's time to pack it in. And take the .22." He pointed to the corner by the door. "The .22 long rifle shells are on that little shelf up above. Just put a few in your pocket, in case you need to use it."

Jack knew what he meant as far as the rifle was concerned. A large animal still in a trap couldn't be finished off with a blow from the hatchet. And it had been a good winter for wolves and coyotes.

"I'll carry the rifle," Cyril volunteered. "You carry the shells." When they got outside, he was confused about which way to go. "Where are the trap lines?" he asked, looking at Jack.

"They must be out back." Jack pointed the way after tying on his snowshoes. "We didn't cross any trails on the way, did we?"

The trap line trails were there, leading out along the little river and its winding valley. Every forty or fifty yards, there was a smaller branch of the trail where a trap would be, off to one side or the other. They had collected almost three dozen small traps, none of them set, when they came to a loop in the trail that looked like it hadn't been traveled for some time. It led upward, and looked like it might be for one of the bigger traps.

"There aren't any more beaver traps out, are there?" Cyril asked, nodding toward a flat area and a swamp.

"No. He only had six of those. They were in the cabin already. I think it's too late for beaver now, anyway."

"That must have been the last beaver Dad was working on," Cyril said.

They'd come to the first of the large traps. They found a coyote that was still alive. The animal looked beautiful, worn out, and defeated, all at the same time. It made little effort even to snarl, as Cyril handed the Cooey rifle to Jack and then stood aside as Jack finished it off. It was a beautiful animal that was on the verge of starvation.

"It looks like it's been here for days," Jack said, as he began the task of skinning it out, while Cyril got busy with the chain and wire that had held the trap and its victim to a big cedar tree. He knew they wouldn't be back that way again, assuming the trap line made a loop back to the cabin or other trails.

"Were you crying back there?" Cyril asked a little farther on. "It's only a coyote, and a good-looking pelt. It would have raided other traps."

"Maybe," Jack admitted as they trudged on. "Killing might be necessary, but it's not fun."

That was all he said as he picked up their pace. He didn't know how long this loop might be, or how many traps they might find. What he didn't say was that he'd seen the look of that coyote before. He'd seen it in his father's eyes.

It was after nightfall when they got back to the cabin. There had been one other coyote and five more traps to bring in. The coyote had been dead for some time. Jack wondered how long it had been since his dad had checked on that long trap line. He wondered about a lot of things.

Even with the evening cooling down so quickly in the dry air sliding down from the mountains, the heat in the cabin seemed almost stifling to Jack and Cyril. But their father still looked cold.

Malcolm had put on some tea for them all, and Jack opened the small sack with biscuits and dried meat that he and Cyril still had. He shared it all around, saving one biscuit each for the next day. He hoped it would be cold enough for easy traveling, and that the wind from the west wasn't the beginning of a Chinook.

"What do we still have to do?" Cyril asked.

"Well," Malcolm coughed and cleared his throat, "you boys can probably pack up and head out with most of the things first thing in the morning. I just want to check the beaver traps one more time. They would have been hard for you to spot."

"How many coyotes and wolves did you get this winter?" Jack asked, almost immediately. "We brought in two more this afternoon."

"It'll be more than twenty," Malcolm answered. "There were also two that we shot earlier on, remember?"

A little bit later, Jack and Cyril walked out along the trail, probably a lot farther than they really needed to, to pee before turning in for the night.

"Didn't you say he only had six beaver traps?" Cyril whispered hoarsely. "Then why does he need to check on the beavers in the morning? Those traps are already hanging in the cabin."

"Because he's sick," Jack said. "And I don't think he wants to leave."

"You mean, here? Not yet?"

Jack wondered if he might already have said too much. He knew Cyril would worry, and he would certainly not be able to keep things a secret if he told him all he knew, or thought he knew.

"I don't know," Jack lied. "I just don't think he can walk too far or too fast right now. And I don't think he wants to tell us he's been sick. Didn't you hear him coughing?"

"Is that why those coyotes had been out there so long?"

"Probably. Come on. He'll be wondering what we're doing." Jack headed back to the dull glow of the cabin. They picked up some firewood on the way.

Sleeping that night was not very comfortable in a small cabin intended for one trapper. Jack and Cyril found a corner to sleep in among some pelts. Their dad's bunk didn't look like it was much better. Malcolm blew out the tallow candle and crawled under a rabbit-skin blanket.

Jack remembered sharing a bed with Cyril when he'd had a cold. But the kind of breathing noises and sporadic coughing coming from under the rabbit-skin blanket that night sounded far worse, and ominous. Only Cyril seemed to be oblivious, as he slept well after a long day's work.

Jack got up a couple of times or more to add wood to the tiny stove, but its warmth did little to help him sleep. He hoped morning would come soon. Then, in almost the same instant, he hoped it wouldn't. He was more than a bit apprehensive about the next day. He feared for a confrontation in which he might have to be the man of the house.

The last thing Jack was aware of in that fitful night was thinking about the small sledge he'd seen outside—two runners of bent hardwood saplings and a platform held together with rawhide. He'd assumed that his dad had used it to haul things around on the trap lines. He thought of wet beavers. And he wondered if it might be big enough to haul other things. It was mostly downhill back to the house.

Malcolm was the first up in the gray of dawn. Maybe it was always gray inside the little cabin. His noise with the stove woke up the boys. Water was soon on for tea.

"Do I get to eat my biscuit now, or do we wait for later?" Cyril asked as he blew vapor off his tea. He'd recently acquired a considerable ability to eat almost anything, and at any time.

"Later," Jack suggested. "We should get packed up first. Right, Dad?"

Malcolm nodded. "Just the furs," he said. "A lot of things can be left behind until the spring. You know, traps and things like that. I'll help bale up the rest of the furs for you."

Jack didn't want to say it, but he knew he had to. "What do you mean, bale them up for us?"

"So you can go ahead and start back. I ..." Malcolm started hesitantly. "I still want to check the beaver traps, like I told you. I might have missed one."

"Dad, your traps are all here, I counted." Jack tried not to sound defiant. He looked down as he said it. Then he looked over at Cyril, wondering if he realized what was happening—that this was a mutiny. He hadn't warned him because he didn't know it might turn into this kind of confrontation.

But Malcolm did. Maybe he'd expected it. "Cyril, go to the river and get some more water," he ordered. And when Cyril hesitated, he added, "Now!" A yell that made him cough and snarl for some time.

Jack didn't know whether or not Cyril was out of earshot, but he began anyway. "Dad, I know what you're doing. And I think I know why."

"You don't know anything yet, boy!" The redness of anger was rising in his face. Malcolm knew that Jack knew. He also knew that saying it would make it seem worse. He looked at Jack and wondered how long he might have known, and what he might have said to Rose, or even to Cyril. "This is between you and me, isn't it? He made it sound as much like an order as a question. "Between the men of the family. Right?"

Jack nodded, looking straight at his father. "It's like on the river last summer, isn't it?" he asked.

It was Malcolm's turn to nod. And, once again, Jack saw the look of the coyote in the trap from the day before.

"Are you dying?" Jack asked. "Or are you going to do it to yourself?"

"Does it matter? Either way, you'll be free." Malcolm looked around and pointed. "There's more fur than ever. It'll be a new start for all of you."

"But we need you to build the scow." Cyril had come in behind them.

"You were supposed to get water!"

"I forgot the ax," Cyril stammered, crying. "The hole froze overnight."

"What did you hear?" Malcolm coughed.

"Are you going to die, Dad?" Cyril asked through his tears. "Do you want to die?"

"What do you know about dying, anyway? Everything dies sooner or later. Some things die so others can live. Where do you think your food comes from? Or the money to buy things?" He kicked feebly in the direction of some of the furs and bales of pelts in the corner near the door.

"But that's what animals are for. I remember Mom telling us that, when we read a story in one of our readers," Cyril began to explain.

"And being sick doesn't mean you have to die, does it?" Jack added. "We've all been sick and got better. Don't you just have to try to get better? Can't Mom make some medicines for you?"

"Sometimes you get sick and you don't get better," Malcolm said, trying to end the conversation. "Sometimes you get hurt and don't get better."

Jack knew there was a lot more that could be said, and maybe needed to be said. He also knew Cyril wouldn't be able to hear and understand those things.

But Rose did need to hear. "You can't just leave it to us to go home alone and explain things," Jack said, looking straight at his father, looking at him man-to-man, challenging him. "We know too much, and Mom doesn't know enough. You're the one who needs to explain it to her, not us."

They sat down in silence for a while. Jack checked the fire and wondered if he should put some more wood in the stove. But that would only put off leaving. Malcolm tried to lean back against the wall, but a fit of coughing pulled him forward again, head down.

"We only have the picture," Cyril stammered. "We don't know how to build a scow, or anything."

"No, not yet. But you would have figured it out," Malcolm said. "That's why I was ready to trust you with it." He tried to lean back again. "Maybe we need to have some more tea first, and talk about that."

The sun was well up into the trees by the time they had talked and packed up what was necessary. The little sledge was big enough for most of the bales and pelts to be strapped onto it. And they had talked about scows and boats that had been on the Athabasca and other western rivers a long time ago. Just in case.

They also talked about death and dying. Cyril had a lot of questions about that. He surprised himself by not crying.

Both Jack and Cyril seemed to be satisfied when Malcolm told them that death wasn't all that hard. That what really hurt was thinking about it and wondering how it would happen. Malcolm looked at Jack at that point, knowing that the two of them understood. They had been there together, on the Athabasca.

Finally, Malcolm seemed to be resigned to the fact that doing it at home was either his punishment or his responsibility, for having brought his family into this wilderness with him. He looked at the hides and pelts. He wondered what death might have been like if he had stayed in the cabin with the wolves and coyotes lurking outside. His feeble laugh turned into a wracking spell of coughing.

All three of the Whyte men knew it would be a long walk home that day.

Most of the weight was on the little sledge that seemed to glide along surprisingly well. Jack and Cyril alternated pulling it. Neither argued about the bulk or the weight. Malcolm said he could at least carry his own pack and the Cooey rifle. The person with the sledge set the pace.

It was almost dark, and at least a mile or more from home, when Cyril spoke up. "There are shadows among the trees."

"They've been getting closer." Malcolm wheezed and coughed. "They can smell the furs, and they probably sense that I'm sick, and ..." He didn't finish. He knew that Jack at least knew how wolves hunted.

"What can we do, Dad?" Jack asked. "Can you move any faster?" But he knew the answer even as he asked it.

There were maybe six wolves in the pack. They were moving with a purpose, and they were getting closer.

"Take the gun," Malcolm said, holding it out to Jack. "They only want the weakest, the slowest, or a cripple."

"Dad?" Jack asked, baffled by the implicit suggestion.

Malcolm almost laughed. "No," he coughed. Then he explained. "There's too many to let them get close enough to shoot and kill them all. This Cooey's good, but it's only a single shot. Can you shoot one in the hindquarters? You know, enough to cripple him?"

"Yeah, probably."

"They only want a cripple. They don't mind if it's one of their own." Malcolm coughed, bending forward, pointing Jack toward the closing shadows.

Jack took aim.

"Paff!" The shadows scattered at the sound of the gun.

"Did you get one?" Cyril asked.

Jack didn't answer. He wasn't sure. But the answer came soon enough—wild, primitive thrashing, moving off into the darkness of the winter forest.

"Move!" Malcolm ordered his boys. "They may be hungry and they may be dumb. But they're not stupid."

He didn't cough again until they saw the lights of the house. "Remember," Malcolm told Jack and Cyril, "I've just got a bad cold. What happened out here," and he pointed with a sweeping wave of his arm, "is between the three of us."

24

A week or so later, Malcolm whispered to Jack, "Sometimes you get a second chance at life, sometimes you don't. Last summer was my second chance with you. It was long enough to be the best part of my life."

It had been a week of futility. A week filled with more love and conversation than all the years before. And sometimes you don't have to say very much for it to mean a lot. That week also made it easier for Rose to answer or explain things later to her children.

Afterward, she used words like bronchitis and pneumonia. But what they heard and understood was when she said, "His lungs were sick. They were probably sick since the war."

"I think the war made him sick in many ways," Jack added. "And I don't think he ever really understood just how much."

25

The ground in the foothills of the Rocky Mountains in the Athabasca River country of Alberta stays frozen until a week before grasses sprout and flowers begin to bloom. But funerals can't wait that long.

Jack remembered a big spruce that had blown over, roots and all, near where they had cut the trees for their lumber. He explained his idea to his mom and she agreed.

"When we sawed up the extra logs a few weeks ago," Cyril mused, "I never thought it would be for this."

"Maybe Dad knew we might need some practice before we started on the scow." Jack welled up when he said it. He also knew his dad understood the practical aspects of life and dying, as he and Cyril nailed together a long box out of some of their extra lumber.

It took a lot of pushing and pulling, and the final use of Malcolm's little sledge, but after a half-hour or so, they had gotten to the tree that Jack remembered. Amelia wondered why the big crosscut saw had been strapped to the top of the box, but decided that, under the circumstances, it was probably better not to ask.

"Well, this is it," Jack said quietly, as they stopped beside the uprooted tree.

Rose nodded and helped the boys slide the box into the big shadowy hole under the upturned roots, that looked oddly like a crown. Then they all worked together to pack snow around and over the coffin box, adding their tears as they did so.

Finally, Jack looked over at his mom and asked, "Okay?"

Rose nodded and drew Amelia to her side.

"We'll have to undercut it first," Jack told Cyril as they picked up the crosscut.

They made two cuts, side by side, into the bottom side of the big horizontal tree, at about where the stump would normally be. They took a rest, and then began to cut into the top side of the trunk, over the undercuts. They worked slowly, rhythmically, stopping frequently, as they worked their way downward, looking and listening for when the top of the tree would fall away from the stump.

"Get ready to jump back when I do," Jack warned, and two pulls later he did just that.

The big tree that had been horizontally suspended, groaned, squeaked, and shuddered. Then the stump, with all the roots and all their dirt, parted from the tree itself and, more slowly than anticipated, but as completely as planned, settled silently over Malcolm Whyte's coffin.

Jack looked over at his mom, nodded, and then embraced Cyril and Amelia, while Rose read the story about love in the 13th chapter of 1st Corinthians. This time, he thought he understood more of what it said. Especially the part that said, "When I was a child, I spoke as a child, I understood as a child, I thought as a child: but when I became a man, I put away childish things."

"Mom," Amelia asked as they trudged back home, "why did you shave off Dad's beard?"

"It's what he wanted, dear. He wanted to look like a soldier one more time."

"But he wasn't wearing a uniform."

"No. But he was wearing the uniform of his life."

A few days later, a Chinook wind sucked away most of the snow, as a prelude to the real spring that was to come later. It was enough to provide a work area close to the house, for Jack and Cyril to begin the work on their scow, while Rose and Amelia began to deal with the cleaning up and drying of the last of the pelts.

Inside the house, on the dog-eared calendar, Rose had arbitrarily selected March 15, circled it, and marked, "Scow begun." In the box a week before that, she had marked a cross and written, "Malcolm."

"We need to have a date for the authorities," Rose explained to Amelia, when she asked about it one evening.

"Will we be in trouble because Dad died?" Cyril wondered.

"No," Rose assured him. "Trouble only happens when you do bad things. Sickness happens naturally."

"Trouble, like accidents?" Cyril asked. "Dad thinks, or thought, that's how Mr. Harley died in the flood. But he wasn't sure."

"But we do have his cat." Amelia said. "And his kittens."

Rose decided it was time to clear the table. Dealing with bobcat kittens or cats might be a situation best left to a future date, when there would be other distractions.

The cleared table gave Jack and Cyril some room to look at the plans for the scow, and decide on their work for the next day. They only had a little room, and only for a while, because the table was also the sewing center for the dresses on which Rose and Amelia had begun to work again.

Spring would be busy, even without a garden and trapping gear to think about.

"Why can't we just use the canoe paddles?" Cyril wanted to know.

"Because Dad said we need oars to move something this big," Jack said with authority, tapping the well-worn drawing they called their blueprint. "And this is a good day to find some trees for them."

Even though it was already April, according to the calendar and Rose's calculations, the winter weather seemed to have retuned. Much of the snow had already melted, but what was left had frozen as hard as rock, making it easy to walk back into the bush to look for some tall, slender trees that could be made into oars and poles for a scow. Along the way, or maybe because Jack had planned it that way, they turned aside to look at their father's grave.

"I guess that stump's like a tombstone," Jack said. Although, what he really wanted to see was how the dirt and roots had settled over the box that he and Cyril had made. He was surprised at how well it had all worked. He wondered if his dad would be pleased. He imagined he heard a cough and a laugh.

"Do they care if Dad wanted to kill himself?" Cyril asked. "You know, maybe have an accident?"

"What? What are you talking about?" Jack sounded angry.

"I heard you and Dad talking back at the trapping cabin that morning," Cyril said by way of explanation. "Do the people Mom needs to give his death date to care that he might have thought about it?"

"Everybody thinks crazy things sometimes," Jack said. "It's only when they do them that it matters."

"Was Dad crazy to live out here? And bring us out here?"

"Why are you talking like this?" There was no doubt about Jack's anger now. "Why do you even ask?"

"Something I heard in Hinton last summer. People in the store talked about the crazy river people when they thought I couldn't hear them." Then he asked, "Is that what they're going to think about us when we get to Edmonton?"

Jack started walking on, looking up for trees that they might carve into big oars.

"People can think what they want," Jack told his brother. "All I know is we've got to try. If we stay here, there'll be nobody left to bury us but wolves. Come on!"

Epilogue

The bobcat kittens hardly noticed that the Whytes had left. They had enough to do, hunting rodents around the little log homestead above the Athabasca River, to keep themselves fed and busy in their natural state. Harley and the orange kitten, Samantha, learned to ride a scow down that river and to keep clear of the oars and poles, and all the activity required to keep the scow in the deeper currents, especially through the section called the Gooseneck rapids.

The scow held all that was important to Rose and her children. After all, they had come with very little eight years earlier. The furs of their last winter's harvest had priority. Their value at auction would determine how much they would have, to start a new life in Edmonton.

Jack's arm was healed, but its slight deformation was enough to keep him out of active military service in the next war. He wasn't disappointed.

Cyril and Amelia were enrolled in high school in September. Cyril had a new and different story about the interesting scar on his right cheek whenever anybody asked. Nobody believed the story about pirates.

Amelia started high school with all the enthusiasm of any student at that academic milestone in life. She borrowed at least two books from the library every week.

Rose found a job for that first summer, but went back to school in September. A school on Jasper Avenue needed a teacher for Grade 6.

Ten years later, Jack and Cyril borrowed a canoe and traveled down the Athabasca from Hinton. They stopped for a while at the place where they had learned something about being the man of the house. They decided not to take pictures of what was left of the house, but did take one of a spruce stump that was slowly giving way to rot.

They finally pulled out near a mill at Whitecourt. It was far enough.

War ends with the death of its last veteran. Only then does it really become history.

Afterword

The Athabasca River has its beginnings in the glaciers that flank the Yellowhead Pass in the Rocky Mountains of Canada. It eventually flows into Lake Athabasca as part of the Arctic watershed. The Yellowhead Pass is one of the lowest through the Rockies, and the northernmost one through which the railway first forged its way in the late 1800's.

Today, the tourism town of Jasper nominally marks the beginning of the turbulent Athabasca, as it tumbles through scenic rocky gorges, before flowing out through the forested foothills. And, near its outflow into Lake Athabasca, it flows through the oil sands around Fort McMurray. Along its modern length, railways and highways cross it; lumber and oil industries are scattered along either bank, competing with farms for economic priority.

In the period between the two World Wars of the last century, the Athabasca was largely the same as it had been in the centuries before. Its surroundings were still as wild and rugged as they had been during the days of the fur trade, when Fort McMurray and Jasper House were well known to the voyageurs. But the transcontinental fur traders were gone in the 1900's. The railways had displaced their raw and basic activity. Farmers and industries were coming in their wake. Only the Great Depression seemed to slow them down. But only for a little while.

It was during that period, between the Wars, that the Whyte family retreated to the banks of the Athabasca to escape from the problems of the world. Or from their own.

Jack, the oldest boy in the Whyte family, couldn't even remember if that had been in 1931 or 1932. Not knowing that was probably another reason for his adolescent anger, confusion, and all that follows.

Acknowledgments

To credit some people for their influence or assistance in this would mean leaving out, or forgetting, many more. Something excusable, I suppose, during this stage of retirement. The forgetting thing, that is.

However, there is one distinct memory.

It was with great foreboding that those of us in North Bay Teachers' College in the mid-1960's entered into Miss Thorn's classroom for the first time. We had heard that she was the very epitome of her own name—precise, to the point, and more. And all of our expectations, or fears, were realized under her tutelage in that year of preparation for our own turn as teachers.

We learned what we respected; we were guided by her precision; and we were encouraged to realize that we, too, could learn more and more. Teachers, after all, should never stop being students themselves.

But, most of all, what she imparted was a love for language

and the art of communication in whatever form that might take.

These qualities were also seen in the editorial staff of Red Deer Press—(Peter Carver and Penny Hozy).

So, thanks to them, and those whose names are possibly forgotten but whose influence continues.

Interview with Harry Kleinhuis

What led to your wanting to tell this story?

Three people were the basis for this story. Jack and Cyril were neighborhood kids back in the fifties. Jack was a young teenager. Cyril was his tag-along little brother. Jack was the oldest in the family and expected to be exemplary in all that he did. It was an expectation that was beyond anybody's talent or ability. Jack used to say that he often got beat for being less than expected. I heard that kind of "event" happen one Saturday afternoon. Jack had failed at something, again. He emerged from the house and his father's punishment, looking stoic, confused, angry, and staring straight ahead, already anticipating the next encounter. Cyril was the one who cried on Jack's behalf. But only briefly.

Joe, a stoic individual who worked with my dad, was not connected to Jack and Cyril in any way. He was a loner, an electrician. I watched him ply his trade, so to speak, helping to re-wire and upgrade our house. All by himself, he wrestled with wires and a brace and bit to bore the holes where those wires needed to go. On a summer day, it was a hot, sweaty job. And the harder it was, the harder Joe worked. Worked, as if pursued by some tireless demon. As a kid, I helped by fetching things for Joe from time to time. But, really, I was there waiting for something to happen. Joe had a reputation. Something that people called shell shock. Something to do with his memories of being in the war. Something that often led to peacetime explosions at work and elsewhere.

You clearly know a lot about the Athabasca country. How did you come by this knowledge?

The rivers in the foothills of the Rocky Mountains rattle and hiss through the gorges and channels they've carved out over the centuries. For a few years in the late sixties, I taught in a school situated on the North Saskatchewan River, about forty miles west of Edmonton. Canoe trips were a part of the school's curriculum, usually following the routes of fur traders—the voyageurs. One of those trips was down the Athabasca, over to Lac la Biche, and then along some more sedate, meandering prairie rivers. We pulled out at La Loche. The beauty of traveling along a river like the Athabasca in the foothills is that, because of the river's deep valley and rugged nature, there is little to see of the farming and other economic activity up above and beyond that valley. Here the rivers exist in natural isolation.

These rivers create and ensure their own isolation by seasonal flooding, sometimes rising into the trees well above their banks.

Malcolm is a man who has been permanently damaged by fighting in the First World War. Do you think all those who take part in such conflicts suffer from such trauma? I had the privilege of being the padre to the local Canadian Legion for a few years. The vets were interesting people. And the older the better. They all had stories to tell, but they never talked about the things they did at the front. Their favorite stories, or memories, were about when it was all over—when countries had been liberated.

As padre, I was involved in a lot of ceremonies and a lot of funerals. The following poem I wrote is a reflection on one of those events.

> *Tribute To A Comrade*
> A paper poppy—
> Such a simple thing
> To lay upon the flag-draped coffin
> Of a friend
> Whose deeds the world had long ago forgotten.
> But, in the figure bent

And stooped beneath the gravity

Of that long, solemn moment,

Was seen an honest tribute

In that last silent eulogy

To a fallen comrade ...

What had their memories shared?

Was it the knowledge of near death

In the savage chaos on a now forgotten hillside

Where flesh and blood

Were the cost and price of each square yard?

Was it, perhaps, the memory of fear

So rich that it brought home

Some men no longer men

But only hollow bodies,

And hands no more equipped

To do the work that peace demanded?

And yet, how could I know?

Or we, or all the world

Who from a grave so easily return

While in his solitary silence

Alone

A comrade mourns

The Whyte family has been living in isolation for seven years when we meet them in this story. They have come to depend on each other for everything, yet they never clearly express their love, even affection, for each other. Why do you think that is?

In the stories of Tevya by Sholem Aleichem (which led to the musical, *Fiddler on the Roof*), Golde asks her husband, Tevya, "Do you love me?"

What follows is a litany of all the work and things they have done together, or for each other, over their many years of marriage. At the end, after all of that, Tevya rhetorically asks, "Why talk about love right now?"

Love is not in saying the words, but in living the life of marriage and family. At times it seems like an obligation but, ultimately, as with the Whytes, love exists in promises fulfilled.

During the time Jack and his father are camping along the river while the boy recovers from his broken arm, he sometimes realizes he's not experienced in making conversation, even though he is fifteen years old. What does he mean by that?

As a result of the Whytes' isolation, Jack hasn't had any experience talking with people—the family is his only society. And, within the family, he is further isolated by being the eldest of the three children. He's trapped in the "no man's land" between his parents and his younger brother and sister. He's becoming a man on his own. Like the young eagles, he knows what he's becoming, but just doesn't know how to get there. And his dad hasn't been any help in the process because he had also been denied that mentoring process, because his own father had died and left him to be the man of the house.

At one point, Malcolm suggests that those who didn't take part in the war can't have any idea of what it was really like. Yet countless memoirs and novels about wartime continue to appear. Do you think Malcolm was right?

Dime novels of the old west, apparently, were often written by people who had never been west of the Mississippi. Their tales were romanticized legends. Such stories exist about war as well. However, to really know something about anything, you have to do it—you have to be there. You get to know a river by going up it as well as down, and for more than just a few miles. You need to do more than just cavort in a shallow set of rapids on a sunny summer day—although, that might be a good place to start.

What do you think Jack will have learned from his father after the family leaves their isolated home on the Athabasca River?

Jack is introspective and reflective. In the same way that he watched the eagles, he will look back on what his father was, and the things he did, and begin to realize why it all happened. He will also realize that in looking back on his father, he will begin to see a reflection of himself.

What is your message to young writers who have stories they want to tell? How important is it to have one's work published?

Writing is the simple process of walking in someone else's shoes and using your imagination to do it. One step at a time, and you're walking. One word at a time, and you're writing.

It's surprising how far you can walk in one day, or paddle.

And getting published is a bonus.

Thank you, Harry, for your insights.